1944
from same
Christina

DICK DONNELLY
of the
PARATROOPS

Story by
GREGORY DUNCAN

FIGHTERS FOR FREEDOM Series

Illustrated by
FRANCIS KIRN

WHITMAN PUBLISHING COMPANY
RACINE, WISCONSIN

Copyright, 1944, by
WHITMAN PUBLISHING COMPANY

Printed in U. S. A.

All names, characters, places, and events in this
story are entirely fictitious

CONTENTS

CHAPTER		PAGE
I.	Token Resistance	11
II.	A Man With Two Names	20
III.	Wadizam Pass	37
IV.	Encircled!	50
V.	Break-Through!	69
VI.	Special Mission	86
VII.	Not So Happy Landings	106
VIII.	Two Visitors to Town	120
IX.	Uncle Tomaso	132
X.	The Old Bell Tower	150
XI.	Fruitless Search	168
XII.	A Visit to the Dam	181
XIII.	The Fourth Night	193
XIV.	Interrupted Performance	207
XV.	No Calm Before the Storm	222
XVI.	Zero Hour	235
XVII.	Aftermath	245

LIST OF ILLUSTRATIONS

Planes Swept Low Over the Airfield	10
"I Want to Get to Fighting," Tony Said	23
"I Want to Stamp Out the Rotten Government."	33
Dick Just Missed the Big Boulder	45
The German Read the Report and Gave an Order	57
Dick Handed Max a Ball of Cord	71
Dick and Max Walked Happily up the Hill	81
Major Marker and the Men Went Over Their Plan	93
Jumping in the Darkness Was No Lighthearted Task	109
Slade Set Scotti's Broken Leg	123
The Two Men Walked Toward the Villa	135
The Old Man Told of the Underground's Activities	145
"By Golly, I Think We Can Get Away With It!"	157
Dick Tied the Rope Securely Around the Box	171
Dick Scanned the Report of German Troop Movements	183
"If I Could Only Get a German Officer's Uniform!"	197
"I Didn't Need to Come Along," the Lieutenant Said	209
Scotti Looked After the Others	225
Dick Stopped Behind a Tree and Waited	241

Planes Swept Low Over the Airfield

DICK DONNELLY
of
THE PARATROOPS

CHAPTER ONE

TOKEN RESISTANCE

The big transport plane flew out of a cloud just as the sun appeared over the flat horizon of the desert to the east. The rolling hills over which the clouds hung low smoothed out as they met and merged with the flat wasteland. A row of trees, the only ones in sight, lined one edge of a rectangle even flatter and smoother than the land near by. A long, low building near the trees, with two small airplanes in front of it, identified the rectangle as an airfield.

Before the transport reached the field, another slid out of the cloud. Suddenly swift fighter planes darted past them, swept low over the airfield with machine guns splattering their bullets over the hard earth, the two small planes, and the low hangar. They circled swiftly, just as a third transport appeared from the clouds, and roared past the field, on the far side of the line of trees. Long streaks of white smoke poured from them, falling lazily and billowing into man-made clouds as dense as those in which the planes had recently been flying. In five minutes the smoke screen was a wall twenty feet thick and a hundred feet high.

Meanwhile, the first transport had circled the field, dropping lower. Suddenly a figure plunged from the side of its fuselage, hurtled toward the ground, and then checked its descent with a jerk as a white parachute billowed out above. Another figure had dropped from the plane before the first 'chute opened, and now it too floated gently to earth behind the smoke screen. In rapid succession, eighteen men leaped from the plane, which sped back toward the hills as another came in to discharge its cargo of soldiers.

As the first man landed, he rolled over the hard earth, tugging at the lines of his parachute to spill the air from it. In a moment it had collapsed and the man had slipped from his harness. Dropping his emergency 'chute, he unfolded the stock of his sub-machine gun and ran forward, crouching, toward the smoke screen, on the other side of which lay the airfield building.

"Jerry!" a voice called from behind him, and he turned.

"Okay, Dick?" the first man called back.

"Yes, sir," replied the second, running up. "And here come the rest."

In less than three minutes the eighteen men from

the first plane had gathered near their leader, Lieutenant Jerry Scotti.

"We won't wait for the heavies," he said. "I think this is a setup. Come on."

He turned and ran into the cloud of smoke, followed by the others, who held their guns ready. As they broke out of the cloud on the other side, they dropped to the ground. The hangar was not more than a hundred feet away. There was still no sign of activity in or around it. Not a man had been seen since the planes first came over.

"No cover here at all," muttered the second man, Sergeant Dick Donnelly.

"No opposition, either," laughed the Lieutenant. "Can't see a soul."

"Think they've skipped out?" Donnelly asked his companion.

"No—no place to skip to, except by plane," Scotti replied. "They must be in the hangar, just waiting. The Major said we might not meet any defense at all. Most of these Frenchmen are mighty happy to have us invading North Africa."

"Sure, but some of 'em are putting up a fight," the sergeant said. "They're good soldiers and if their officers tell them to fight back, they fight back."

"Get back a bit into the protection of the smoke," Scotti said, and his men pushed themselves back ten feet. "Now let's give them a burst and see what happens."

The silence, broken only by the steady drone of airplane motors in the skies overhead, was shattered by the stuttering explosions of sub-machine guns. The bullets thudded into the thick, hard clay walls of the hangar.

Suddenly three rifles and a pistol were thrust through the windows at the rear of the hangar and they fired repeatedly—*into the air!* Then a white flag was thrust from the middle window on a long pole, so quickly that it must have been ready for the purpose.

"We surrendair!" called a voice from the hangar. "Les Américains—zey have conquered us!"

"All right," shouted Lieutenant Scotti, advancing from the smoke screen about ten feet. "Toss all guns out the window."

"Oui, oui, at once!" came back the voice.

Half a dozen rifles, three automatics, and two light machine guns were thrust from the windows and clattered to the ground. By this time two other groups of American soldiers had appeared, one to the right and one to the left of Scotti's group.

"It's all over," he called to them. "Hold your fire! They've surrendered."

"My golly!" cried a voice from the group on the left. "What did we come along for—just to take a ride?"

But Lieutenant Scotti had turned his attention back to the hangar.

"Now come out that side door," he called. "One at a time, with your hands up."

In a moment the side door of the hangar was opened and out stepped a smiling French officer, his hands in the air. His blue uniform was as trim as his tiny mustache, and he walked erect, with dignity and military precision. Just as the other French soldiers came out behind him, three men appeared from the smoke, which now was lifting somewhat, behind Scotti's group. Dick Donnelly turned from his officer's side and called to them.

"Take it easy, boys," he said with a grin. "The heavy machine guns won't be needed—unless you want a little target practice later just to keep in trim."

The men, who had quickly assembled a machine gun dropped by parachute from one of the planes, rushed it forward with all possible speed, stopped in their tracks, dropped their heavy burdens, and looked disappointed.

"Aren't we *ever* gonna get any fightin'?" grumbled the first man.

"Wasn't that little business at Casablanca enough for you?" asked Donnelly.

"Sure, but that was three weeks ago!" was the reply.

By this time the French soldiers were lined up alongside the hangar, their hands in the air. There were two other officers, four enlisted men and four men whose overalls showed that they were mechanics.

"We have resisted," cried the first officer happily. "Did you not see? We fired our guns in resistance against your attack as we have been commanded. But your superior numbairs overcame us. Yes?"

Lieutenant Jerry Scotti grinned and walked forward.

"Sure, I understand," he said. "You put up a whale of a fight! Lucky nobody was hurt. You can put your hands down now."

Scotti turned to his sergeant.

"Sergeant Donnelly, you may send up the flares signaling capitulation of the French airfield after a brief but fierce fight. The other planes can come in now."

As Dick Donnelly, with a few of his men, hurried off to carry out the Lieutenant's order, Jerry Scotti extended his hand to the French officer, who grabbed it and shook it heartily, mumbling happy phrases all the time in such an outpouring of words and exclamations that Scotti, whose French was limited, could understand nothing of what was said. But he did know that the man was delighted—so delighted, in fact, that a mere handshake would not suffice to demonstrate his enthusiasm. He flung his arms around Lieutenant Scotti, who looked a little embarrassed, especially at the grins of his own men who stood in a circle around him.

"I feel as if I ought to say something important," he muttered, "like 'Lafayette, we are here' or something."

The other groups of soldiers had gone forward to the hangar, searched the inside of the building, looked over the two obsolete French fighter planes standing in front, and watched Donnelly set off his signal flares. In a few minutes they were looking at half a dozen more transport planes as they circled and came in for a landing on the hard runway of the field. Their wheels had hardly stopped rolling when men in khaki uniforms piled from them, formed lines and were marched to the edge of the field by their commanding officers.

A half hour after the first plane had appeared from the cloud over the hills, there were two hundred American soldiers at the French airfield. In the hangar, Lieutenant Jerry Scotti saluted Captain Murphy, who came in with the air-borne troops, and made his report.

"Good work," the Captain said, as he sat at the desk and began to look over the papers on it. "The transports will take you and the other parachute troops back to your base at once. They have to get off the field within ten minutes because the fighter squadron will be coming in. We've leap-frogged quite a jump this time. Oh yes—see that the French prisoners are taken back to your base, too. And you can tell them they'll probably be fighting alongside us against the Germans within a few weeks."

"They'll like that, sir," Scotti said. "I've talked with a couple of them. I've never had anyone so happy to see me as they were. Still, they had to put up that token resistance."

"Yes, wonderful spirit," Captain Murphy agreed. "You can inform Captain Rideau, the commanding officer, that his actions when we attacked the field will be relayed to the French authorities who will organize French forces in North Africa to battle the common enemy."

Within two hours, Lieutenant Scotti, Sergeant Dick Donnelly, and all the paratroopers from their plane as well as the others, were back at the little town which had been their base for the past week. The Frenchmen, technically under military arrest, had the freedom of the town.

At dinner that evening Private First Class Max Burckhardt complained loudly to Sergeant Dick Donnelly.

"What a washout!" he grumbled. "Nothing but a nice plane ride, an easy parachute jump, a little standing around in the hot sun, and then a ride back again. Do they call this a war?"

"Keep your shirt on, Max," Sergeant Dick Donnelly replied with a smile. "The French *want* us to come. Just you wait until we make contact with the Germans!"

"Ah—yes!" boomed the burly private. "That's

what I'm waiting for—for a chance at some of those Nazis."

"It won't be long now," mused the sergeant. "It won't be long."

CHAPTER TWO

A MAN WITH TWO NAMES

As the days rolled by, the good-natured complaints grew in number and intensity. The men wanted to fight and they were not fighting.

"When I volunteered for the paratroops," young Tony, the radioman, said one day, "I did it because I like action. I like excitement. I like thrills. Danger—it doesn't mean much to me. Some day I'm gonna get killed, that's all. I'm sort of a fatalist, I guess. When my number's up it's up, and sitting around worryin' about it won't change it. Meanwhile, have a good time, get a kick out of things, and do your darnedest in anything you've got to do."

"I know what you mean," Dick Donnelly said. "And I feel a little bit the same way—but I don't believe in not ducking when a shell's coming over."

"Oh—I don't invite death to come see me," Tony said. "But, as I was sayin', I thought the parachute troops would be wonderful. And important, too. Droppin' behind enemy lines, messin' up their communications, blowin' up a few bridges, takin' an airfield—and all this with the enemy all around you! It's good tough stuff, and that's what I like. But what happened?"

"Well, what *did* happen?" Dick smiled.

"I get into the parachute troops after my basic," Tony said. "And then, first, they teach me how to fall down. As if I haven't fallen down plenty of times when I was a kid. And from places just as high as they made me jump off of, too. When you're a kid duckin' away from the gang from the next block, you know how to climb and dodge—and fall. Then the practice jumps from the tower! What do they need a tower for? Why not just get us up in a plane and toss us out? We'll learn how to use a 'chute fast enough that way, don't you worry."

"But, Tony, you've got to remember," Dick said, "that not everybody is as agile as you are. And they don't have the same attitude as you. They feel a little funny at first, jumping out of an airplane. And they're likely to get mixed up and forget which side the ripcord is on. Some people tighten up and get panicky. They've got to learn things slowly, get used to them."

"What's so hard about it?" Tony demanded. "You jump, and you don't even have to worry about the ripcord. It's hooked inside the plane."

"Well, they've got to teach you how to land right," Dick countered. "Otherwise you might break a leg or get dragged half a mile by your 'chute."

"Anybody knows he ought to roll when he falls," Tony said. "And you can see you have to spill the air out of your 'chute and slip out of the harness. It's easy."

"For you, yes," Dick said. "You could scramble up the side of a sheer wall twenty feet high, like a cat. You'd have made a wonderful bantam halfback if you'd ever played football, Tony, the way you can duck and dodge and twist and go underneath or over anything that's between you and where you want to go. Anyway—so paratroops training was easy for you. Then what?"

"One thing I did like," the young corporal said, "and that was the conditioning. They decided paratroopers had to be tough and they put us through everything to make us tough. I like that. I like to be hard as nails and in perfect condition all the time. It makes me feel swell. And I liked the chance to learn radio. I'd fooled around a lot with it as a kid. The Army really taught me things about it."

"And you learned what they taught, too," the sergeant said. "That's why you're a corporal so early in the game, and so young."

"I don't care about that," Tony said. "I want to get fighting. I don't like this sittin' around. I thought this North African invasion would really be the works. When we shipped out from home, I knew it was something big. But what have we done?"

"Tough fight when we landed back of Casablanca," Donnelly said. "That was a good scrap."

"I Want to Get to Fighting," Tony Said

"Sure, it started off fine," Tony agreed. "But then we just sat for three weeks. Sure, we moved forward from one base to another as the ground troops went forward. But no fighting. No parachuting. Nothing. Then today we thought it had come at last. But it was nothing. Just a practice jump."

"When we reach Tunisia," Dick said, "we'll run into some real fighting. By the way, Tony, I suppose you've thought some about how you'll feel fighting Italians. Will you be so anxious to fight them?"

"Well, I'm an American," Tony said. "I was born in America. I'm fighting for America. But my folks —they were Italian. And their friends, lots of 'em come from Italy. And I've got cousins and uncles and aunts there, even visited them once for almost a year when I was about sixteen. But it's not them I'm fighting. They don't want this war at all. They're fightin' just because somebody is makin' 'em do it. That's why they've been so lousy during this war. Some people think I must get upset when Italians always run away in battle. No—I like it. It doesn't mean they're cowards or bad soldiers. It just means they don't want to fight *this* war."

"Well—I don't want to fight, really," Dick said. "And neither do most Americans. What about that?"

"You don't like to go to war," Tony said. "Neither do I. But we know what we're fightin' for. We know our country's worth fightin' for. But what about these Italians—most of 'em? They haven't got anything to fight for—against us. They love their country, but not their government. And they know they'll get shot or starved to death, or their kids will get punished some way, if they don't fight when the government tells them to. So they fight—but without any heart in it."

"But you may be killing some of them," Dick said. "Maybe even some of your relatives."

"That'll be too bad," Tony said. "I don't want to kill anybody, really. But if you've got to shoot a few guys, or even a few million, because some louse who wants to ruin the world has sold them a bill of goods or made 'em go out and try to kill *you*—then that's just the only way to do what we've got to do. When I shoot at the enemy I'm not shootin' at any one person. I'm just shootin' at an idea I hate, an idea that will ruin the whole world if it isn't stopped. If the other guys are supportin' that idea with guns, then I've got to shoot 'em, that's all. And it doesn't make any difference if they're Italians or not. It doesn't make any difference if they're Americans. If any Americans try to make our country like Germany, then I'll shoot them too."

Max Burckhardt had wandered up and joined them as they sat under the shade of a palm tree.

"Tony's right," the big private said. "But I'm itchin' especially to get at some Germans, even if my folks were German. I won't be shootin' Germans—I'll just be shootin' the men who are tryin' to force on me their way of living, a way I don't like at all. Since the German Nazis did this more than anybody else, they're the ones I want to get at more than anyone else."

There was a moment's pause.

Dick Donnelly sighed. "Well, you'll have your chances soon," he said. "Both of you. You'll be fightin' Germans and Italians before long."

"Say—by the way," Max said, "I found out what Lieutenant Scotti's first name is."

"Why, it's Jerry, of course," Dick said. "We've known that right along. I always call him Jerry, except when a lot of officers are around, and then I've got to use *sir*."

"Well, Jerry's just his nickname," Max said.

"Don't tell me it's for Gerald," Tony said. "It just wouldn't fit that guy."

"No—remember his last name," Max said. "His folks—or at least his father—was Italian back a couple of generations. The name is Scotti. And his first name is Geronimo!"

"Geronimo!"

Both Dick and Tony cried out at once, and sat up, looking with disbelief at Max Burckhardt.

"You're kidding!" Dick said, shaking his head. "Why, that's what we yell when we jump—to overcome the sudden change in pressure against our ear drums. And just because the lieutenant's a paratrooper somebody's called him Geronimo as a gag."

"No, it's really official," Max insisted. "I was over at headquarters gabbin' with Joe Silcek while he pecked away at his typewriter. I saw it on an official list."

"An official list?" Donnelly said, concern wrinkling his forehead.

"Sure—what's wrong?" Max asked. "I wasn't lookin' at anything I shouldn't. It was right there —everybody's name on it in our company."

"Oh, everybody's," Dick said, and was silent.

"What's the matter, Sarge?" Tony Avella laughed. "You act as if you'd been caught travelin' under a phony name and Max had found you out."

"Me?" Donnelly tried to laugh it off. "What an idea! You couldn't travel under a phony name in the Army."

"Say, I've always wondered about that name of yours, anyway," Max said. "Didn't want to say anything until I knew you better. But you really look as Italian as Tony here, and I know you speak Italian like a native. How come the Irish name?"

"Well—it *is* an Irish name!" Dick said. "You see —my mother was Italian."

"Oh, and your father was Irish?" Max asked.

But the sergeant just grinned. "I might as well come out with it," he said. "No—my father was Italian, too."

"Then—where did that name Dick Donnelly come from?"

"It really was Irish in the beginning," the sergeant smiled. He looked out over the rolling hills and watched the heat waves rising from the flat lands. It was pleasant here under the tree, talking to his friends. The war seemed miles away, and yet the war had brought him friends like this, brought him a whole new life. And now that old life was going to come out. If they all hadn't been so restless between battles, his old life could have stayed buried. It wasn't that Donnelly was ashamed of it, but just that he wasn't sure the others would understand.

He was silent, as he thought about it, and the others waited, knowing he was going to tell them something interesting about himself. Their relationship was not the ordinary one of sergeant and lesser ranks. In the parachute troops, men were often thrown closely together when they worked frequently from the same plane, always in the same group. Commissioned officers were more informal and friendlier with the men under them, too. Lieutenant Scotti and Dick Donnelly, for example, were very close friends. They kept to the formalities only in military matters, but in private they called each other "Jerry" and "Dick."

Dick Donnelly liked Max Burckhardt and Tony Avella. He had been with them at training camp and ever since. They would be going through a lot more together. So it was natural that he should tell them about his other name, his other life.

"Donnelly's an Irish name, all right," he said. "And that was my family's name originally. You see, there were quite a few Irish settled in Italy a few hundred years ago and they just switched their names to the nearest Italian equivalent. My Italian name is Donnelli, of course."

"Why did you switch to Donnelly when you came in the Army?" Max asked.

"I didn't switch then," Dick replied. "You see, my folks were crazy about it when they first came to America. They made up their minds to become as American as George Washington. So they changed the name back to its old original, Donnelly, because it sounded more like most names in America."

As Dick talked, Tony Avella was looking at him closely, with a puzzled expression on his face.

"Dick Donnelly," he murmured to himself. "Richard Donnelly!" And then a light dawned in his eyes and he smiled. "I get it now! I thought your face looked a little familiar. Of course, I've seen pictures of you. I've seen you—and heard you, too!"

"What is all this?" Max Burckhardt demanded.

"Am I right?" Tony asked, smiling at his sergeant.

"Yes, you're right, Tony," Dick answered.

"Say, let me in on the secret," Max blurted out.

"Sure, Max," Tony said. "Just translate Richard Donnelly into Italian. Ricardo Donnelli."

"Sure—sure—Ricardo Donnelli," Max said impatiently. "That's obvious, but what does—"

He stopped, and looked at Dick Donnelly in awe. "My golly, are you really—" he mumbled. "Are you *the* Ricardo Donnelli?"

"I guess I am," Dick grinned. "I haven't run into any others."

"The famous Metropolitan opera star!" Tony cried. "And we've never heard you sing a note!"

"Well, I didn't think many people in the Army would be very interested in the kind of stuff I sing," Dick said.

"Say—I've stood back there with aching feet at the Met so often," Tony said. "I've waited in line for those standing-room tickets just to hear you sing. And now I've been your pal for months and you've never even warbled!"

"No, I haven't really felt like it," the sergeant said. "I started getting upset about this war long before we were in it. My folks hated fascism since Mussolini first started spouting in Italy. I wanted to join the Loyalists in Spain but I was just getting started in my singing career then, and felt I couldn't do it, after working so hard for the chance I finally got at the Met. I've been seeing it coming for a long time, and when I finally got a chance to fight I joined up and forgot everything else. I'm no Ricardo Donnelli any more. I'm Dick Donnelly, paratrooper in the United States Army!"

"You studied in Italy, didn't you?" Max asked.

"Sure, everybody does if he gets a chance," Dick said.

"Why is that?" Max asked. "America's got plenty of good singing teachers, plenty of good music."

"Sure, but not the way it is in Italy," Dick explained. "You see, in Italy there are little opera companies all over the place. Every town has its own opera and its own orchestra. They're not like the Met, of course, but there are dozens of them which give a newcomer, an unknown, a chance to sing. And that's what counts—plenty of singing in public, on an actual stage, in a real performance. I sang in half a dozen small companies in my two years in Italy. And somebody noticed me and gave me a chance at La Scala in Milan, and there somebody from the Metropolitan heard me and signed me up. Of course, when I had come to Italy to study and sing, it was natural for me to go back to my old Italian name, Ricardo Donnelli. So I've stayed Ricardo Donnelli as far as singing is concerned."

"Why didn't you ever let on who you really were?" Tony asked.

"Well—several reasons," Dick said. "As I told you, I'm not concerned with singing now, but fighting. I'm Dick Donnelly. And then if they knew who I was, I'd always be asked to be singing here and there, at shows and camps and such. Then like as not I'd find myself transferred to some morale-building branch of the service just going around building soldiers' morale by singing operatic arias. And I'd get no fighting done at all. I got into this war to fight. I want to stamp out all the rotten government I saw in Italy when I was there—and its even worse versions in Germany and Japan—and everywhere."

"I see," Tony Avella replied. "I feel pretty much the same way, not thinking about anything but this job we've got to do. So I won't go spouting around that you're Ricardo Donnelli, the great singer. But if we're ever alone out in the hills at night, will you sing *Celeste Aïda* some time?"

"I sure will, Tony," Dick answered with a warm smile. "If I can still sing."

"I'll keep my trap shut, too," Max said. "If you want to be just Sergeant Dick Donnelly, then you can be it. You see, I had an uncle and aunt in Germany that I loved a lot. They didn't like Hitler and they said so. They were that kind. And they're dead now—died in stinking concentration camps. So I'm not thinking much about anything, either, until I get even for them. It's going to take a lot of dead Nazis to make up for Uncle Max and Aunt Elsa."

"For a bunch of guys who say they want to fight so much," Dick laughed, "we seem to be taking it

"I Want to Stamp Out the Rotten Government."

pretty easy, sitting here in the shade on a nice afternoon."

"The whole outfit's goin' nuts," Tony said. "All anxious to get into the thick of it. It seems as if our gang is just about the blood-thirstiest in the Army. That's why they all joined up with the parachute troops—thought they'd get first crack at the enemy if they dropped behind their lines."

"We've got quite a cross-section in our own plane," Dick said. "We've all got special reasons, the three of us here, for wanting to fight and fight hard. I suppose most of the rest of them have too. There's Monteau, the Frenchman. He doesn't say much, but from the look in his eye I'd hate to be a German meeting up with him. And there's Steve Masjek. He's a Czech, and you know what those boys think of the Germans. Barney Olson's got relatives in Norway. And there's a bunch of just plain Americans with no special ties to the old world who are pretty anxious to fight, and fight some more."

"But *when?* When?" cried Max. "I thought I was itchin' to get at those Nazis, but I guess we've got one gent in our outfit that's more anxious than I am. Did you hear about Vince Salamone?"

"No, what about the home-run king?" Tony asked. "And say—that makes me think, we've got a fair representation of boys whose families came from Italy—the lieutenant, Scotti, and Salamone the baseball player, and myself—and now you, Maestro

Donnelli."

"Sure—the Army knows we're going to invade Italy," Dick said. "We're going to come in handy. But what about Vince?"

"He got picked up trying to hitchhike to the front," Max said. "Just flatly stated that he didn't want to be a paratrooper any more 'cause he hadn't had a real chance to fight yet and he had to have it. Other boys were fightin' up front, he said, and he aimed to help 'em out instead of sittin' around here waiting for an airplane ride."

"What did they do with him?" Dick asked.

"Oh, the Major acted sore, of course," Max said, "because he had to. But he really liked the guy's spirit. And everybody likes Vince anyway, not just because he's the best ball player in the world, but one of the nicest guys, too. He got three days in the guardhouse and no furlough for a month, that's all."

"Well, he won't miss anything," Tony said. "It's no duller in the guardhouse than here, and there aren't any furloughs these days, anyway."

"He's going to miss *something*," a voice said from behind the group chatting in the shade of the tree. They all sat up and turned around to see Lieutenant Scotti. Quickly they jumped to their feet and saluted. Scotti saluted in return and then ambled up to them amiably.

"Yes, Salamone is going to miss a little action," the lieutenant said, "and you guys who've been itching to get into action so badly have at last got a chance to do a little fighting. And—this is for you especially, Private Burckhardt—we'll encounter a few Germans!"

CHAPTER THREE

WADIZAM PASS

"We're really just a diversionary action, a feint," Scotti said, his voice raised slightly so that all the men in the plane could hear him above the muffled hum of the plane's engines.

"So we're not gettin' into the real thing even yet?" Tony Avella demanded.

"It's the real thing, all right," the lieutenant replied, "if it's tough fighting you want. We'll have plenty on our hands if plans work out right, because we'll draw off a sizable force for our main group to pinch off."

The men all leaned forward eagerly.

"You see, the Germans have holed up in the Wadizam Pass, and that's on the main road to Tunis and Bizerte," the lieutenant continued. "We've got to break their hold there and that's no easy job. The planes have been giving them a pasting from that French field we took last week, but they've got plenty of cover and have stood up under it well. A frontal attack is almost suicide because our men would have to march between hills covered with German guns."

"This begins to sound like something," Dick

Donnelly commented, and several others nodded, waiting for Scotti to continue. It was one of the things they liked most about their lieutenant—his willingness to tell them as much as he could about any action they were going into. Lots of men had to fight almost in the dark, but Scotti felt his men could fight better if they knew why they were fighting and what they were up against.

"Two Ranger companies have been walking all night over mountains with almost no trail," Scotti said. "They've probably been running, instead of walking, as a matter of fact, because they had fourteen miles to cover, over rough terrain, in complete darkness. Think that over while you're sitting here nice and comfortable in your private airplane!"

"Where are the Rangers going?" Max Burckhardt asked.

"They're cutting over the hills, to come down on those entrenched Germans from above," Scotti continued. "The Germans won't expect it for a minute. In the first place, the hill is considered almost impassable. Also, their observation planes have not noted any move of a body of troops in that direction. That's because the troops waited for darkness, were rushed to the bottom of the hill by truck after dark, and will climb all night. It's an almost impossible feat, and the Germans don't think we're very good soldiers yet. They think you've got to have plenty of battle experience to do a job like that. So they're sure we won't pull such a trick."

"Well—I know those Ranger-Commando boys are good," Dick Donnelly said. "But *can* they really do it, if it's so near to impossible?"

"They'll do it," the lieutenant replied with a smile. "They had the whole job put up to them on a volunteer basis, and the toughness of it wasn't played down, either. And they were told that we fellows would be sticking our necks out, because our very lives depended on their making that march on time. They said they'd make it, and they said it as if they meant it. They know the score— and they won't miss."

Jerry Scotti looked around at the faces and saw smiles, a few nods, and some relief. These men knew, too, that the Rangers would get to the top of their hill on time, even though many of them would be carrying guns and mortars.

"Okay—now here's where we come in," Scotti said. "Just after dawn we fly past the Wadizam Pass, to the north of it, circling around as if we were trying to sneak in just when we had enough light to see but before the Germans would see us. Of course, they *will* see us and we know it. But they haven't got much of an opinion of us as soldiers or tacticians yet; so they'll think we're fools enough to believe we can get away with it."

"I get it," Tony Avella said. "They've been saying the Americans were stupid. Well, we're going to take advantage of their thinking that."

"Sure, that's it," Scotti said. "And we'll be quite a parachute force dropping behind their lines on the opposite hill from the ones the Rangers will be coming over. Twenty planes dropping paratroopers back there can cause a lot of damage, and they know it. There're a couple of important bridges, a dam, and some telegraph lines we can cut."

"Is that what we're going to do?" Dick asked.

"No, it's not," the lieutenant answered.

"I didn't think so," the sergeant said. "We'll want to be using that dam and those bridges and lines pretty soon ourselves."

"Right," Scotti agreed, and went on. "But the Germans will have to send back quite a good-sized force to round us up. First, they'll want to do the job fast, before we could do much damage, so they'll send a big force. Next, they know we'll have good cover in the hills, and they'll be coming up the slope to get us. To do that the attacking force has to be about four times as strong as the defenders. And in this case, we're the defenders, holding the hilltop."

"We can mow 'em down," Max Burckhardt grinned.

"Sure, we can," Scotti said, "for a while. And then they'd overcome us with greatly superior numbers and a few fairly heavy guns they'd trundle up there in a hurry. But they won't get that chance. If we can draw off 1500 to 2000 men from the main force at the entrance of the pass, they'll be weakened by more than a third. Then the Rangers swoop down on them from their side—flanking them so their biggest guns are not in position to return fire. It will be a complete surprise to them, and at the crucial moment the main force will attack at the front."

"Sounds fine—if it works," Tony muttered.

They all agreed, but no one said what would happen if it did *not* work. They all knew that if the attack failed, the paratroop force would be cut off completely, surrounded and mopped up.

"So, even if we're a diversion," Jerry Scotti smiled, "I think we'll get in some pretty good fighting. Tony, I'll want that radio set up in a big hurry."

"Right you are, sir," the young man replied. "I'll have it going in ten minutes after it lands, if you'll detail a couple of men to help me get it out of the 'chute containers and put together in a good spot."

"Sure," the lieutenant replied. "MacWinn and Rivera—you help Tony with the radio first. There won't be any shooting for a while, anyway; so you won't miss any of it."

Suddenly, after all the talk, there was complete silence in the plane. The men were all looking into space, or at the floor, thinking, picturing what might come in the dangerous action ahead of them. The plane purred on steadily. This was always the most difficult time, Lieutenant Scotti knew. That was why he so often passed the time telling his men about the coming action. The ride in the plane just before they jumped and began to fight—that was when hearts beat a little faster, when men's throats felt a little dry.

"It's just about getting light over to the east," he said quietly, and the men looked up. The co-pilot stepped through the door from the cockpit at that moment, and spoke to the lieutenant.

"About three minutes," he said. "All set?"

"All set," Scotti replied with a smile, and got to his feet. Before he could utter his command, the men were on their feet attaching their long ripcords to the cable that ran the length of the fuselage over their heads.

"Got 'em trained, haven't you?" the co-pilot commented. "Don't have to give them any orders."

"Not this gang," Scotti replied. "They know what to do better than I do."

The men all smiled at that, pleased with themselves. They weren't tense any more. The time for real action was here at last, and they were ready for it.

The side door was opened, and the men braced themselves against the blast of air that swept against them.

"Remember—low jump, men," Scotti said. "Okay —go ahead, Dick."

Clutching the Reising sub-machine gun across his

chest, Donnelly leaped into space with a shout. But to the customary "Geronimo!" he added the word, "Scotti!" But the lieutenant did not hear, for the blast that caught Dick swept him thirty feet from the plane by the time the second word was out of his mouth. And Scotti was already giving his curt order to the second man to jump.

In rapid-fire order they went, piling out of the plane only two seconds apart. When the last man had jumped, Scotti and the co-pilot grabbed up two large containers with parachutes attached and tossed them, with the lieutenant following them immediately.

Dick Donnelly was swinging slowly and gently at the ends of his shroud lines. He looked below at the rocky and uneven ground covered with little clumps of short, scrubby trees. He reached up over his right shoulder and tugged at the lines a bit so that his body shifted to the left slightly. He was picking his spot for a landing.

Then he stole a glance upward and behind him, smiling with pleasure as he saw the sky filled with scores of white parachutes.

"Looks like a snowstorm," he muttered to himself. "They sure did pile plenty of us out in a hurry over a small area."

The planes had already swung westward as they climbed away from the first ineffective bursts of antiaircraft shells from German batteries to the south. There was no German airfield in the Wadi-zam Pass—it was too narrow and rocky—but they would be radioing for fighters to the field at the rear, over the hill.

"The transports will get away, though," Dick mused. "They're just about out of ack-ack range now, and the fighters will be too late."

He looked down at the ground again, which suddenly seemed to be coming up at him more rapidly. When the parachute first stopped his descent, it seemed almost as if he were floating in the air, settling downward, ever so slowly. But as he neared the earth, he had a better estimate of the speed at which he was traveling. With a last glance upward at the many white 'chutes interspersed with a few colored ones bearing machine guns, mortars, radio, and ammunition, he slipped his 'chute lines once more and got ready for the rolling fall.

"Going to miss that big boulder all right," he told himself. Then his feet touched the earth and jolted him as he tumbled sideways and slightly forward, yanking vigorously against the shroud lines on one side.

But he did not have to worry about the escape from his parachute, for it caught against the boulder he had missed, and collapsed. Quickly he jumped to his feet, slipped out of the harness, ditched his emergency 'chute, and looked up toward the crest.

"Yes, there's the ledge," he said to himself, and

Dick Just Missed the Big Boulder

ran forward, the loose gravel and rocks rolling down the steep hill behind him as they were kicked loose.

The ledge toward which he was running was a broad and sweeping shelf in the side of the hill, only about a hundred feet from the crest. It extended all along the ridge and was perhaps fifty feet deep at most points. On the northern end it narrowed to nothing where the hill dropped sharply down in a precipice to a small valley below. At the southern end the ledge just merged gradually into the hill itself. It was here that it would have to be defended. No enemy troops could hope to attack from the north, up the cliff.

In less than two minutes, Dick Donnelly had reached the ledge and was giving it a quick glance which took in all details, when more men streamed up the hill to join him. They all looked it over just as Dick had done, noting at once the big boulders that could give good cover, the depressions out of which good foxholes might be dug, the occasional overhanging rocks which made half-caves. Then their glance swept down the hill, seeing which way the Germans must come when they did come.

Tony Avella, with MacWinn and Rivera, struggled up the incline with their big boxes. With only a short glance, Tony motioned his men to follow him up beyond the broad ledge, nearer the crest of the hill. There, Dick saw him motion toward a big boulder which lay near a clump of the low, rugged trees. They dumped their boxes, and Tony started to open them at once.

Dick turned to direct men who arrived with heavy machine guns. The first carried the gun itself, the second its tripod mount, the third the water-cooling apparatus for it. Not far behind them climbed four men with boxes of ammunition for the gun.

"There—between those two big rocks at the edge," Dick said, pointing. "You can get a straight sweep down there."

With a grunt the men moved to the spot designated by the sergeant and began to set up the weapon with swift movements that wasted not a second or a bit of energy. Then Lieutenant Scotti stood at Dick's side.

"Okay, Dick," he said. "Nice spot, isn't it?"

"Perfect," Dick said. "We could hold off an army here for days, provided they didn't come at us from over the crest behind our backs."

"Not much chance," the lieutenant replied. "No roads or trails on that side of the ridge at all. It would take them a day and a half to get around there, and it ought to be all over by this afternoon. They'll not even get a chance to think of it. But you forget about planes."

"Yes, you're right," the sergeant agreed. "Not a good spot for planes. They can get at us pretty easily. But our own—"

"They're going to be pretty busy," the lieutenant

said. "They'll be disrupting roads and supply lines behind the Pass and helping out the Ranger attack and then the frontal attack. They'll help us if they can, if the Jerry planes come after us."

Within ten minutes after the parachute landing, the entire force was disposed, with machine guns emplaced, and mortars in position behind them. Men were digging foxholes out of the rocky soil, selecting spots beside boulders for the maximum protection. Lieutenant Scotti had reported everything to Captain Marker, in command of the operation, who had set up headquarters almost at the crest of the hill. It was an exposed position, but it offered a perfect observation point.

"I'll be able to see the Ranger attack when it comes," the Captain pointed out, gesturing toward the hill on the opposite side of the valley. "They'll be streaming over there as soon as we give the word. Is the radio set up?"

"Yes, sir," Scotti replied. "Corporal Avella is ready to go at any time. We're to use the call letters indicating that we're communicating with our main base, but the Rangers will be picking it up on their walkie-talkies on the opposite hill."

"That's right, Scotti," the Captain answered. "And now you'd better get those details headed out for the dam and other spots they'll be expecting us to go after. The enemy will probably have observation planes over here in a few minutes and we've got to carry out what will look to them like an immediate threat to their dam and communication lines. Then they'll hustle a sizable force here."

"Yes, sir," the lieutenant replied, saluting as he turned and went down the hill.

He found Sergeant Dick Donnelly directing the placing of boxes of ammunition for the machine guns.

"Sergeant Donnelly," he called.

"Yes, sir," Donnelly replied, stepping to his side.

"I've got a job for you, Dick," Scotti said quietly. "And not an easy one."

"That sounds good, Jerry," Dick replied. "What is it?"

CHAPTER FOUR

ENCIRCLED!

"Here's a map of this region," Lieutenant Scotti said, unfolding a paper which Dick Donnelly looked at eagerly. "You can see the hill we're on. Here's the pass in the valley below, and over there is the hill over which the Rangers will attack on the flanks. They're probably waiting under cover there now."

"Yes, I see," Dick replied.

"Well, back here is the dam," the lieutenant said. "We've got to make a pass at it, as if we were going to blow it up. Also, we've got to send out parties as if to cut this telegraph line over here, and another as if to blow up that bridge on the road out of the pass. As you know, we'll not do any of those things, but we want the German observation planes—which ought to be coming along in about five minutes—to see us heading in those directions. They'll report back, and the commander in the Pass will rush up at least a third of his force to stop us."

"I get the idea," Dick said. "And which one do you want me to go after?"

"I thought that's what you'd say," Scotti smiled. "I want you to take twenty men and head for the dam. That's the most dangerous of the three missions. As you can see, the telegraph line is not in an exposed position, and it's not so important as the other points. If the Germans get any force around there in time, it won't amount to much and our men can get back here fast without being cut off. The bridge is harder, and the Germans will want to save that. But their force can really come at it from only one direction and our men can just back up the hill here, fighting them off as they do it."

"Yes, I can see that," the sergeant said.

"But the dam's a different matter," Scotti went on. "In the first place, they've probably got a squad or two on guard there, with radio. So you'll have to make a feint at a real attack to make our bluff work. But most important, the Germans can come on you from both sides and encircle you without any trouble."

"Sure—you can see that from the map," Dick said. "That's what they'd do right away. But if we had a walkie-talkie with us, you could let us know in time, and we could sneak back out of the trap and get back here."

"But we can't do that," the lieutenant said. "You'll have a walkie-talkie all right, and we'll keep in touch with you. But you and your men have got to keep the German detail pinned down there as long as possible. You've got to get yourself surrounded and hold them there, while we're holding the main force on this ledge. You've got to hold them long enough so they can't be rushed back to help stem the Ranger attack. We'll give the signal for the Rangers to pour over that other hill when we know we've got the greatest number of German soldiers tied up battling us."

"I see," Dick replied grimly. "We get ourselves surrounded. We hold the attacking force there. Our chance of getting out is either to hold out until relief comes to us, after the main battle of the Pass is over, or to break through the encirclement ourselves and make our way back here."

"That's the idea, Dick," Scotti said. He didn't like the idea of giving this toughest assignment to one of his best friends, but he had to put a good man in command of the dam detail, and Dick Donnelly was the best.

"Let me study that map a minute," Dick said.

Scotti handed him the paper and watched the sergeant note carefully every detail around the dam. Suddenly he put his finger on a double line leading away from one side of the reservoir and asked, "What's this?"

"That's an ancient Roman aqueduct," the lieutenant replied. "You see, back in the days when Rome ran this part of the world, they had a dam here, supplying water to the cities to the east. That aqueduct led from the reservoir across the little valley there and then followed the line of the hills eastward."

"Is the aqueduct still standing?" Dick asked.

"Part of it, anyway," the lieutenant replied. "Let me speak to the captain to see if he knows any more details."

Scotti and Donnelly moved to the little switchboard under the lee of a rock and the lieutenant spoke to the commanding officer on the crest of the hill. When he had finished, he turned to the sergeant.

"He says that our observation photos show it to be intact," Scotti said. "And they were taken only a couple of days ago. A couple of the supporting pillars are crumbling a bit at the bottom; so we've no idea how strong it is. But it's all there, at least across the valley after it leaves the reservoir."

"That's all I wanted to know," Dick said.

"I believe I know what you're thinking of," Scotti smiled. "Of course you'll be approaching the reservoir from the other side, where the modern dam is."

"Sure, I won't be anywhere near the old Roman aqueduct," Dick grinned. "—maybe. May I pick my own men?"

"Sure, as long as you don't take Tony Avella away from his radio," the lieutenant said.

"Okay—twenty of 'em?"

"Right. Hop to it."

Scotti turned away as Dick Donnelly headed for the group of men from his own plane. He went from one to the other asking each one first if he wanted to volunteer for a good tough job. When each one eagerly said, "Yes," Dick next asked how well the volunteer could swim. He questioned each one earnestly as to just exactly how well he could handle himself in the water. Then he picked the men who were sure they could swim well. Max Burckhardt was among them, pointing out that he had been swimming instructor at a boys' camp for several years when he was younger.

"Will I get the most fighting going with you or staying here?" Max asked.

"With me," Dick replied. "Even though it will be plenty hot here. We'll probably be outnumbered about forty to one."

"Then count me in," Max said, "and I'll get my forty!"

"We travel light," Dick said. "Each man with a sub-machine gun and plenty of ammunition. And chuck a few extra cans of rations in your shirt front."

In five more minutes Dick Donnelly had his twenty men lined up. He reported briefly to Lieutenant Scotti.

"We're on our way, sir," he said.

"Got your walkie-talkie?" Scotti asked.

"Yes, and a good man with it," Dick said. "But if things get tough, we may not bring it back with us."

ENCIRCLED! 55

"Don't worry about that," Scotti said. "Just bring yourselves back."

"We'll see you late this afternoon," Dick smiled.

"Right—and good luck," the lieutenant smiled. Then he turned and busied himself with other tasks so that he would not watch Sergeant Donnelly leading his men up over the ridge and down the other side to skirt the cliff-like northern end of the hill. Scotti checked on the groups heading for the telegraph lines and the bridge, and they set off shortly after Donnelly.

"Remember—let the observation planes see you," he called.

Dick and his men had taken a last look down at the American camp on the ledge and had marched on over the crest when they saw the first German plane. It was a little hedge-hopper, flying low and coming from the east. Dick knew that the Germans in the Pass had radioed headquarters about the parachute raid and the observation planes were coming over for a look.

The slope down which they were walking was rocky and bare, so there was no place to hide if they had wanted to. They watched as the light German plane circled overhead and then passed on over the ridge.

"That pilot is radioing right now to the Germans in the pass," Dick said to Max, who walked behind him. "He's telling them a raiding party of twenty men has set off toward the dam."

"And by this time he sees our main camp on the ledge," Max said, "and he's telling them about that. He won't get any very accurate figure of how many men there are there, though. The rocks and ledges will hide some of them."

"Yes, and in a few minutes he'll see the bunch heading for the bridge and the gang going to the telegraph line," Dick went on. "There won't be any doubt about it. There's no place else for raiding parties to go."

Dick's guess was right, for back in German headquarters at the Pass, the commanding officer was scanning the radio reports sent in by the observation plane. He smiled.

"Tell dem to keep track of dese men," he ordered. "Ve send men to vipe dem off der map at vunce. Dey must *not* blow up der dam und bridge!"

The order went out to a subordinate, and men piled from their barracks into waiting trucks. Truck after truck roared up the road through the Pass, heading north. If the commander of the Rangers, in hiding on the west hill above the German camp, had been able to see, he would have been pleased at the number of trucks that scurried away, crammed full of German soldiers.

It was only a few minutes later that Captain Marker, leader of the parachute troops, saw the first of the trucks on the road below, where it rounded

The German Read the Report and Gave an Order

a bend in the narrow valley. He counted them off eagerly, his smile broadening as the numbers increased.

"It's working!" he exclaimed to Scotti, who stood beside him. "They must be sending almost half the force off on this job. They don't expect a thing from the flanks. Just think what a tiny bunch of parachute troops have been able to do, Lieutenant!"

Scotti agreed, but he smiled to himself at the irony of hearing a commander express happiness when his own troops were to be so greatly outnumbered.

"He's not thinking of himself or his troops for a minute," Scotti told himself. "He's just thinking of the success of this operation to take the Wadizam Pass, no matter what it may cost. That's a good soldier, all right."

He watched as many of the trucks sped on out of sight.

"They're going on to get the boys heading for the dam and the bridge," he said. "And they're sending plenty off on that job! The rest will come up after us. Well, we can hold off almost any force in this position for quite a few hours."

Dick Donnelly and his twenty men had been making fast time toward the dam, down the slope of the crest they had crossed, and up the next parallel ridge. Dick looked frequently at his map to check position and glanced almost unconcernedly at the observation plane which returned occasionally to keep them under scrutiny.

"They've probably got a small force guarding the dam," Dick told his men, "and we might as well get rid of them before the detachment from the main camp arrives to take care of us."

He noted with satisfaction that the slopes surrounding the reservoir up ahead were covered with trees whereas the surrounding countryside was rather barren.

"Moisture from the reservoir," he told himself. "Makes a regular oasis here in the hills, and those trees will give us good cover."

As they entered the thicket of trees, Dick stopped his men, who gathered around him. He held the map so that all could see.

"Here's where we are now," he said, putting his finger on a point near the reservoir. "The dam is up ahead on the left a few hundred yards. We've been covered by this shoulder of the hill as we approached, so the guard there probably hasn't seen us, but they're likely to have radio and know we're coming. They'll all be centered at the dam itself, I'm sure. Lefty, you take these five men and head up the hill farther, then cut down to catch them on the flank just after we've gone straight in at them. And Bert, you take these three and circle down around to the left and come up on them from that side. But don't go as far as the road leading from the Pass up to the dam. The Jerries will be rushing a few truckloads of reinforcements up the road to get us, and we've all got to stay on this side."

"I get it, Sarge," Bert said.

"Okay—me too," added Lefty. These two corporals were men who were calm in an emergency and possessed plenty of initiative, as Dick well knew.

"This shouldn't take more than about five minutes," he went on. "And we haven't got much more time than that. The minute it's over, all the rest of us will switch up beyond the reservoir here where Lefty's group is going down, but we must stick close to the shore. We'll have cover, because the trees come right down to the edge. Okay—get going, boys. Wait for my first fire to draw them toward us. Then come in at the right moment."

The ten men who remained with their sergeant watched the other groups trot silently off through the trees in different directions.

"We'll give them about three minutes," Dick said, "to circle around to position. Then we'll go in straight for the dam. But keep behind the trees and rocks. No use losing any men on a little action like this."

Dick looked at his watch as the others stood around him without a word. They held their submachine guns lightly in their arms, ready for immediate action. Dick noticed with satisfaction that they all seemed completely relaxed and at ease, even though a light of excitement and anticipation gleamed in their eyes.

"Okay—here we go," he said casually, and started forward smartly. The men fanned out around him, moving upward through the trees. Dick led them up a slight shoulder of land which brought them to a level with the dam. And then they saw it.

It lay only about seventy-five yards ahead, a long wall of concrete, with water trickling slowly over a spillway at the far end. At the near end there was a rough wooden shack on top of the wall, and near it stood four German soldiers, anxiously scanning the surrounding trees.

"They must be mighty uncomfortable," Dick said, "knowing we're coming for them. Well, let's not keep them in suspense. Open fire."

The silence of the hills was shattered by the chattering roar of ten machine guns. Two of the Germans toppled from the wall to the rocky valley below. One darted into the shack, and one fell on top of the wall, wounded. He tried to drag himself to the shack but collapsed before he could make it. Then from the shack itself came an answering burst of machine-gun fire.

Dick heard bullets whistling through the air and the little snip-click sounds as they nicked branches and leaves. There was a short silence and then another burst from the shack, which was not answered by the Americans. They were busy making their way forward from tree to tree, getting within fifty yards of the shack.

"What about a couple of grenades, Dick?" Max Burckhardt asked. "I've got half a dozen in a bag here. Thought they might come in handy."

"Maybe—" Dick said. "But not yet. Let 'em have it!"

Once more the American machine guns poured their hail of lead into the shack, followed by another burst from the woods to the right.

"That'll be Lefty and his bunch," Dick smiled. "And I guess the Nazis don't like it."

It was obvious they did not like it, nor the third burst from below them on the left. Bert's group had joined the fray. The Germans had Americans on three sides and a large reservoir behind them. It did not take them long to make up their minds what to do. A white cloth tied to the end of a rifle was thrust through the little window of the shack.

"I guess they didn't have many guys there," Max said. "They sure gave up easy."

Dick led his group forward to the edge of the woods and called from there, "All right, come out with your hands up—on to the wall of the dam."

The door of the shack opened and three German soldiers marched out, throwing their guns to the ground and raising their hands as they did so. They stepped over the body of their companion who had tried to reach the shack but failed.

"Is that all?" Dick demanded, with a shout.

"Ya, ya—all, all!" one of the Germans called back.

"Funny—but I don't believe him," Dick muttered to Max. Then he called to the German again.

"Okay, then pick up that machine pistol of yours and fire a few bursts into the shack!"

The German looked bewildered and called back that he did not understand.

"You tell him, Max," Dick said. "Then he can't pretend he doesn't know what I mean."

Max called out the order in German, and the soldiers on the wall almost jumped to hear their own language spoken to them so perfectly.

The first soldier, a corporal, picked up the machine pistol and started to aim it into the shack, but did not pull the trigger. As he hesitated, Max commanded him again to fire into the shack or get a burst of fire from the Americans.

The German soldier looked at the gun in his hands, then at the shack and then at the Americans. Suddenly he fell to the ground, hiding behind his dead comrade and pouring a fusilade at the Americans. At the same moment, two more guns were thrust through the shack window and joined the attack. Dick and his men were quick to get behind trees, despite their surprise. Dick heard a cry of pain from one of his men, but did not take time at that moment to look.

He and his men were answering the rapid crossfire of the Germans, when they saw two dark objects lobbed through the air from the woods on the right. Then there was a roar, a blinding flash followed at once by another, a cloud of black smoke—and silence, as the booming sound echoed among the hills.

As the smoke cleared away, Dick saw that the two grenades tossed by Lefty and his men had done a thorough job. The shack was a pile of lumber, and some of it had toppled to the ground below the dam wall. The Germans who had hidden in the shack during the fake surrender were no more—and neither were their companions alive. Dick and his men advanced on the run, arriving at the dam as Bert's group rushed up from the left. Lefty's men stayed where they were, waiting for the others to join them.

A quick inspection showed that the enemy detail at the dam had been wiped out. And then they heard the sound of motors. First they looked into the sky, but saw no planes.

"Trucks!" Dick said. "On the road below. Come on!"

Even before they moved, they heard the report of rifles from the woods below them. They needed no further warning to make them duck and scurry off the dam into the trees at the right. Skirting close to the shore, they soon ran into Lefty and his group.

"Come on," Dick said. "Over that hump of rock ahead of us. Get positions just over the crest."

The men darted forward, scrambling up over the little hill that came down to the water's edge. Dropping down on the other side, they found cover quickly and faced back in the direction from which the enemy must be coming. They saw that their little hill was a point of land projecting into the waters of the reservoir. It was a good spot Dick had chosen —hard to get at from the direction of the dam itself and not much easier from above, for the hill curved around like a natural fort and the land above was somewhat bare of trees because of the rocky soil. The Germans would have to expose themselves badly if they came from that direction.

Dick looked behind him at the reservoir to see if the lay of the land were the way he had figured it from the map, and he smiled with satisfaction. Opposite the point of land on which they had taken up positions was another point, and only about twenty-five feet of water separated the two. Beyond the two points, the artificial lake opened out broadly.

"They won't come at us from the other side," Dick figured. "The land is too steep to come up that way, and anyway, they'd come directly at us, figuring that they had us encircled with the water behind us."

Then he remembered the cry of pain from one of his men and turned back.

"Say—somebody got a slug back there in the woods," he said. "Who was it?"

"Me, Sarge," said Private Latham, a wiry little fellow who knew more jokes than anyone in the group and so was a favorite among the men. "But it just nicked me in the left hand. Doesn't hurt now."

"Let me see," Dick said, stepping to Latham's side. He saw at once that the bullet had gone through the palm of the hand. Quickly he got out his first-aid kit, dumped some sulfa powder into the wound, bound it up with a bandage.

"Not my gun hand, anyway," Latham said. "I can still shoot."

At that moment they heard the first attack from the Germans. The Americans in position answered with a short burst of fire, knowing that it would pin the approaching Germans down to rocks and protecting trees.

"Got to work fast now, boys," Dick said, as he finished putting away his first-aid kit. "For about five minutes they'll try coming at us directly. Then they'll send out a bunch to come down on us from above. But we can stop them before they get to that bare stretch. Then they'll try crossfire from those two positions, and when that doesn't work, they'll begin tossing grenades and maybe get a few light mortars into action. That's when we'll really get it, and if possible we'll want to get away before then."

"Get away?" Max Burckhardt exclaimed. "How do you figure?"

"Wait and see," Dick grinned, knowing that Max and the others had quickly figured out that they were pretty well trapped, and that they hadn't the ghost of a chance to get away alive. "But first I've got to find out what's going on back in the Pass. If they want us to hold this crowd here as long as possible, we'll just have to do it."

The corporal with a walkie-talkie pack on his back had already pulled up his aerial and turned on his radio.

"See if you can get Tony," Dick said, and the radioman nodded.

"Got 'im," he said in a moment, but his words were almost drowned by the sound of another exchange of bursts between the Germans and the Americans. Dick crept to the ridge beside his men and looked at the woods below. The Germans were really pinned down effectively about a hundred feet away, and the little hill gave complete protection to the Americans. He slid back down beside the radioman.

"He says Nellie went to town about fifteen minutes ago," the radioman said.

"Swell!" Dick exclaimed. "That means the Rangers attacked and the battle is on. What else?"

"Nice tea-party at the Smith's," the radioman went on.

"Good fight at the ledge where we landed," Dick translated.

"Tony winds up with the order 'Show me the way to go home,'" the radioman concluded, and Dick knew that he and his group were free to make their getaway if they could. The battle back at the Pass had progressed far enough so that he did not need to try holding the force at the dam any longer.

CHAPTER FIVE

BREAK-THROUGH!

Lieutenant Scotti smiled. A well-placed light mortar shell had just landed in a cluster of three German trucks on the road below. And that had happened shortly after word had come of the Ranger attack on the remainder of the German force in the Wadizam Pass itself. Everything was going not only according to plan, but even more swiftly and efficiently. The enemy had fallen into the trap completely, splitting his forces so that the Ranger attack could sweep him off his feet.

"I wonder how Dick Donnelly's making out," he thought to himself. "He's in the tough spot and may never get back. Oh, well—"

But at that moment Dick Donnelly was helping four of his best men to fix their sub-machine guns securely between the rocks aiming down the little hill toward the Germans. Two more were fixed so that they aimed up the slope over the bare patch of ground. And these six guns were the Thompson guns with round drums holding fifty cartridges, instead of the lighter Reisings which the rest of the men carried.

The rest of the men continued the fire as the guns

were fixed securely in place. A party of Germans had been sent up around to the right, but they were held to the trees far up beyond the bare stretch. A half dozen who had started a rush across the rocky patch had been cut down before they went ten steps, and the others did not want to share that fate.

"Lefty, Bert, and Max," Dick said, "stay with me at these guns. The others of you shove off into the water. Swim for that other point. If there are any Germans on the dam wall itself, they may be able to see you for about the last ten feet, so make it under water if you can. Drop all equipment, guns, radio and everything except for a few cans of rations. Move—now, fast!"

The men needed no more explanation of Dick's plan. They headed down toward the water as Dick and the three others crouched behind the rocks at the crest of the little hill, keeping up the steady fire. But the Germans were holding their fire more and more, and the lulls between bursts became longer and longer.

Dick glanced around and saw four men already striking out into the still waters of the reservoir.

"The Jerries are probably bringing up some mortars from the trucks below," Dick muttered to Max and the others. "We'd just better hope that they don't get the range too fast, before we get out, too. Here—get these cords attached."

He pulled from his pocket two balls of stout cord

Dick Handed Max a Ball of Cord

and handed one to Max, the other to Bert.

"Tie one end to the triggers of the fixed Tommy guns," he said. "Then reel off a good length, about seventy-five feet, and cut it. Get lengths of cord on each Tommy gun. Keep up our own fire with the Reisings. Give 'em a burst once in a while so they'll know we're still here."

The men carried out the order quickly, as Dick kept glancing back at the men in the water. All were on their way across now, and the first man was reaching the stretch where he might be seen by any Germans on the dam wall.

"I don't think they've got any men there, though," Dick told himself. "Don't see why they should. They know the dam isn't blown up yet, which was their main worry, and they know they've got us trapped back here. Of course, they may be ordered back to the pass to help the main force attacked by our Rangers. But the frontal attack should be started on the Pass by this time, and it might be all over before they could get there."

He was pleased to see the first man duck under the water and swim the last ten feet without being seen. And he smiled to see him come up in the shelter of a rock on the opposite point of land.

"Good going," he said to himself. "He couldn't have been seen even if the Jerries were looking that way."

But his smile vanished as a roaring blast shook

the earth beneath him. Instinctively he hugged the earth, and felt gravel, rocks, and dirt rain down on him from above.

"First mortar shell," he spoke to the others. "Landed just on the other side of the crest. Come on, give 'em a good burst. Get those cords in your hands and let's go."

Before the burst of fire from the Americans ended there was another roar—this time behind them. Dick whirled to see the radio, which had been left on the shore, rise into the air and spread into a hundred pieces along with rocks and earth. Crouching low, he ran down the slope to the shore, with Max and Lefty and Bert immediately behind him. At the shore line he turned, grabbed two of the cords which were hooked to the Tommy guns wedged in the rocks. He gave them a gentle pull, and the others did the same with their cords. The gun chattered from the ledge above them, and they knew the Germans would not try to rush the crest. They'd wait for the mortars to do the trick. As the four Americans slid into the water, still holding their cords, they saw a shell dig a mighty hole in the rocky earth just behind the crest, where they had been not one minute before.

"There go two of the Tommy guns!" Dick said. By this time they were up to their chests in the water.

"One last burst before we swim," he commanded

tersely. He pulled on his two cords. One was limp —attached to one of the guns that had been blown up by the last mortar shell. But the other tugged the trigger, and he heard the stuttering fire it gave forth, along with the other guns that were still functioning.

"Swim for it—and fast!" Dick shouted to his companions.

They heard another roar behind them, then another in quick order, then a third. By this time they were swimming swiftly toward the other point, and it was not far away.

"Don't bother to go under," Dick muttered between strokes. "We don't care if they do see us now."

His clothes felt heavy, like lead weights holding him back. In trunks he could have made the distance in a minute; now each forward push was short. But suddenly he felt his feet strike the bottom, and he pushed forward rapidly up the point of land.

There were no more bursts of shells behind them as they ran for the woods. But just as they plunged into the thick tangle of trees, the chatter of machine guns blazed behind them and the *zing* of shells filled the air. Bert fell to the ground and Max went down beside him. With a quick motion he rolled Bert and himself behind a boulder. There Dick crept up to them.

"Go ahead!" Bert said. "They got me in the leg.

BREAK-THROUGH! 75

They'll be swarming over that stretch of water in a minute."

"Oh, no, they won't!" Dick said. "Remember—we're all picked swimmers. And we dropped our guns. They'll come after us only if they can keep their guns, and I don't think they can manage it with 'em."

Machine-gun bullets still spattered around them intermittently, and they could hear the angry, bellowed orders of a German officer across the water behind them.

"He's telling 'em to cross over," Max said. "He's telling 'em we've got no guns and to go ahead after us!"

"Well, I've got the answer for that," Dick grinned. He reached inside his shirt and pulled out a waterproof pouch. Ripping it open he extracted a service automatic, dry as a bone. Heading around the rock as he hugged the ground, he wriggled forward about ten feet in the underbrush. There, peering through the branches of a bush, he saw the Germans on the opposite point. Standing on the crest was the officer, still bellowing orders to his men, who moved slowly forward toward the water. They didn't like the idea of making that crossing.

Dick steadied his right arm on the ground, aimed the automatic carefully, and squeezed the trigger. The German officer's angry words were cut short. He looked startled and dismayed, as if someone had played an unfair trick on him. His hand went to his chest, he looked around him for a second, and then toppled forward from the ridge, rolling to the shore below. The German soldiers looked at his body a moment, then turned and scrambled back up the little hill as if death itself were chasing them. In two seconds they were all on the other side of the hill. Dick grinned and ran back behind the rock where Bert and Max waited for him. A tentative machine-gun burst followed him, but he was safe behind the rock.

"I don't think they'll come across now," he said. "I got the officer, the one who was telling them we had no guns. At least they won't be coming for a little while, until another officer makes them do it. Come on! Up you go, Bert!"

Max and Dick lifted Bert and carried him rapidly forward through the trees. Fifty feet further along they found the rest of their men, and Dick counted them quickly. Yes—they were all there.

"Jimmy," he said to one of the men, "you take over with Max to carry Bert here. The others will spell you once in a while. I've got to go ahead to find that old aqueduct. Follow me!"

He led the way briskly through the trees, and the men, still dripping from their swim, followed him without a word. They climbed the sloping hill for a quarter of a mile, then cut down sharply toward the shore of the reservoir again. They could see the placid water through the trees ahead when Dick stopped them.

"Wait here while I have one quick look," he said. "Put Bert down, and give him first aid—but fast. Then two others take him when we're ready to go again."

The sergeant moved forward to the water's edge swiftly. In a moment he stood on a huge pile of old rocks which stretched like a wall along one edge of the man-made lake for a distance of about sixty feet. Here was the old dam from the days of the Romans, and stretching away from the wall was the arching aqueduct, spanning a narrow but deep chasm.

"Still standing, all right," he said to himself. "But not too strong. Those pillars look pretty crumbly, but we'll have to chance it. Spread out—then there won't be much weight at one time."

He hurried back to his men in the shelter of the trees.

"How you feeling, Bert?" he asked.

"Okay, Sarge," the big soldier replied, but Dick could see the pain behind his smile. "Sorry to cause so much trouble this way. Don't let me hold you up."

"Rot! You're not holding anybody up," Dick said. "Let's get going. Spread out about ten feet apart going over the old aqueduct up ahead. It may not be too strong, but we've got to chance it. If it's stood all these centuries it can stand another half hour for us."

Dick motioned Max to lead the way, and he stayed behind. Max stepped from the trees, on to the old stone wall and then to the aqueduct. He marched across it at a steady swift pace, and another man started off behind him after he had gone about ten paces. Dick watched carefully. There were three men on the ancient structure—now four. Max was only about ten feet from the other end.

"He's across!" Dick exclaimed, as Max turned at the other end and waved both arms with a smile. "Okay, let Bert and his two carriers go next."

The wounded man and his companions stepped on the aqueduct. Their pace was slower than that of the others, and everyone watched without a word as they made their way slowly forward. It seemed to Dick that he must be holding his breath.

There was almost a cheer from the men as the wounded soldier and his two carriers made the other side of the gully. Then the remaining men, with Dick at the end, followed quickly, without any concern about the old aqueduct.

On the other side, Dick explained briefly the course they would have to follow to get back to their own men. It was a roundabout circle over two ridges of hills, and across one stream that had to be forded. But they felt sure they would meet no enemy forces on the way, as their path covered wild country off the main routes.

The going was slow because the men all felt a letdown after their forced marches of the day. Now they felt safe, sure that they had eluded any pursuing force that might come after them.

"As a matter of fact," Max said to Lefty, "I don't think anybody's following us. Those boys at the dam must've got word of the battle down in the Pass. They're probably heading back down there now. I hope they're too late."

"This was a pretty good shindig, wasn't it?" Lefty commented. "First time we've really had something of what we wanted. We really did a paratrooper's job today."

"Yes—pretty good, pretty good," Max replied, with a sigh. "But I didn't get my forty Nazis. I figure I only got about eleven myself."

"No—you got to look at it this way, Max," Lefty said. "What we did up here made it possible for our boys down in the Pass to wipe out a few thousand. So really you got a lot more than forty."

Max smiled. "I like the way you put it," he said. "But I want to do it personally."

They had a quick meal before climbing another hill, digging food out of their ration cans. When they went on again, Max was walking beside Dick Donnelly.

"Pretty smart operation, Dick," Max said. "You really handled it swell all the way through."

"Thanks, Max," the sergeant replied. "But I was lucky that we were able to get away so soon and didn't have to pin those German forces down for another hour or so. We couldn't have got out if we had had to do that."

"No, but you were prepared for every break we did get, and you took full advantage of it," Max said. "That's what counts. Why they don't make you a general is more than I can see."

Dick laughed. "Wait till I get us back to our forces safely before you congratulate me," he said. "I hope I'm taking you in the right direction."

But Max had no doubts. Dick obviously knew where he was going. And even though the group of men went more and more slowly as the afternoon wore on, it was from nothing but weariness. They knew they would get back to their headquarters under Dick's guidance.

But it was late—almost sunset, when they saw ahead of them the crest of the hill on the other side of which was the ledge where they had landed that morning.

The last pull up that hill was a tough one, and the men grunted as their feet slipped on the rocks. When they were halfway up, they were spotted by an American at the crest, who gave a whoop of pleasure at what he saw. In a moment, others were scurrying over the crest of the hill and running down the slope toward the weary soldiers of Dick

Dick and Max Walked Happily up the Hill

Donnelly's gang. Among the first to reach them was Lieutenant Scotti.

"Dick, my boy!" he shouted. "What a sight for sore eyes! You made it back! And from the looks of you, by swimming, too!"

Dick smiled back weakly. "Yes, sir, we took to the water," he said wearily. Suddenly he felt as if he could not move another step. As long as the responsibility for the detachment had been on his shoulders, he kept his spirits up, encouraged the men to keep going. But now he could relax, and he did. He just wanted to sit down where he was and go to sleep.

Without a word, Lieutenant Jerry Scotti slipped one of Dick's arms over his shoulder and helped him the rest of the way up the hill. Other men had taken Bert in their arms and still others helped the weary Donnelly gang over these last steps.

Over the crest of the hill, they went down to the ledge, where they were surrounded at once by their friends. Dick went with Scotti to report to Captain Marker, who beamed at him.

"To be perfectly honest, Sergeant Donnelly, I didn't expect to see you and your men again," he said. "Yours was almost a suicide mission. Did you bring all your men back with you?"

"Yes, sir," Dick said. "Private O'Leary got a slug in his right leg and Latham one through the left hand. No other casualties, unless you count sore feet. We had to abandon all of our equipment, though."

"Of course, of course," the Captain said. "You've done a fine job, Donnelly, a particularly fine job. And I know you'll be glad to learn that the battle of Wadizam Pass is over. A complete victory! About fourteen hundred Germans dead, two thousand captured. Some few got away into the hills."

"That's wonderful, sir," Dick replied. "How did it go here?"

"Lieutenant Scotti will give you the details, I know," the Captain said. "Now there are trucks waiting on the road below to take us back to the Pass. You men need some rest."

On the way down to the trucks, Jerry Scotti told Dick about the action at the ledge. The Germans had tried over and over again to advance straight up the hill, and many had been cut down. When they unlimbered the mortars, they did a lot of damage, with the Americans losing twenty men in the entire action.

"It would have been worse," Scotti said, "if the Rangers and regular troops hadn't cleaned up the Pass itself so quickly. They sent a bunch up here, and they took the Germans from behind. It was all over in half an hour then."

That night Dick Donnelly slept the sleep of the good and the just—for eleven hours, along with the rest of his men. And the next day they moved back to the parachute troops base.

"Well, that's that," Tony Avella said, as they sat under the shade of a tree. "Best action so far. I guess everybody's happy but Vince Salamone, who sat this one out in the guardhouse."

"Yeah, the home-run king is fit to be tied," Max said. "But I bet he'll be a good boy from now on. He doesn't want to miss another little tussle like this. Wonder what we'll get next?"

Although the men themselves quickly dropped the subject of the Wadizam Pass battle, concentrating their thoughts on the future, it was not so lightly passed over in headquarters in a city behind the lines where a three-star general went over reports of that action with others of his staff.

"That Wadizam Pass action was brilliant," he said. "General Ackerly planned and executed it without a flaw. And I thought it would take us another two weeks to get past that bottleneck."

"Yes, and he had some good men under him," said one of his aides. "That paratroop company really pulled the Germans away with their feint. That's why the Rangers cleaned up everything so quickly. When the frontal attack came, there was almost nothing left to do."

"Captain Marker should get a promotion for that," the three-star general commented. "But what I like best is that suicide squad they sent out to the dam never really expecting to see them again. And they all came back! I'm glad Captain Marker gave us such a complete report on that action. I have an idea we're going to be able to use a crowd like that for some special tasks when we get to Italy."

CHAPTER SIX

SPECIAL MISSION

Dick Donnelly and his friends were not thinking of Italy. They were thinking of more immediate objectives—Bizerte, Tunis, and the driving of Rommel's Germans into the Mediterranean. During the course of that action they were kept a little busier than in their first few weeks. There were no complaints of inaction such as had filled the air previously.

Max Burckhardt missed one battle when he was in the hospital with a touch of fever. Lefty Larkin was killed in another battle, and a few other casualties cut down their numbers somewhat. Bert O'Leary had been sent back to a main hospital for his leg to heal, but young Latham's hand wound had kept him out of only two actions. Vince Salamone, after his release from the guardhouse, had become the greatest battler of them all, making up for lost time with a vengeance.

It was in the invasion of Sicily that the group first met George "Boom-Boom" Slade. He was not a paratrooper, really, but he found himself joining more and more paratroop actions. Slade was a master sergeant and a demolition expert. He knew dynamite and nitroglycerin as well as most soldiers knew their Garand rifles. He knew the construction of bridges, dams, radio towers, so thoroughly that he could place a small blast in exactly the spot that would crack the dam, or demolish the bridge, or topple the tower. Naturally, his constant work with explosives had given him the nickname of "Boom-Boom" and he didn't mind it.

"Funny," he said one day, "but I've gotten so I love blowing up things. You work with something long enough and you get to like it, I guess."

He did not look like a man who would love explosives. He was short and rather slight in build, with mouse-colored hair and a colorless face. The glasses he wore made him look like a rather timid student. He was quiet and mild, a gentle person who liked to feed stray cats and dandle babies on his knee.

But when he set to work at his profession, he changed. Dick Donnelly had been amazed the first time Slade went along with them in Sicily. They were to hold one bridge and blow up two others behind the German lines. Lieutenant Scotti had stayed with the force at the bridge they were to hold for the advancing Americans, while Dick went off with Slade and a few others to blow up the bridges on two side roads.

Dick could not believe that this mild little man could possibly be a demolition expert. In the first place, he hated jumping from a plane in a parachute, but never mentioned the fact. Dick knew it by the agonized expression on Slade's face. Then once on the ground, he acted as if he didn't know where to turn, and just followed Dick around like an obedient, if slightly frightened, dog. But when they reached the first bridge, Slade changed. He stood off and eyed the structure, almost forgetting those around him. Dick had meanwhile placed his men to hold off any German patrols that might chance that way, but he kept his eyes on Slade. In less than two minutes, the little man had decided exactly where the charge of dynamite should be placed, and set at that job with a swiftness and precision that was wonderful to watch. In five minutes more they all withdrew some distance and the bridge was blown up. One end rose in the air about six feet as the other end cracked, and the entire center span fell into the bed of the stream below.

Slade went back for a quick look at his work and seemed pleased. "Good," he muttered to himself. "Our engineers can get another span across there for our own men in half an hour."

That had been the idea—to blow up the bridge so that it could not be used by retreating Germans but could be used by advancing Americans after only a short delay. The Germans would be too hard-pressed by the Americans to take the half-hour necessary for the repair. Foot-troops would be able to ford or swim the stream, but trucks and heavy guns would be caught—and captured!

After the first bridge demolition, Slade, once more the meek subordinate, had turned to Dick, and had trotted along behind as Donnelly headed for the second bridge, two miles away. There had been a short fight there—with four German soldiers left to guard the bridge. Slade wasn't much good in fighting, Dick saw. Not that he was afraid—he was just ineffectual. The other men with Dick were among the best, and the Germans had been disposed of quickly. Slade did an even faster job on the second bridge, and then the whole party had cut back through the woods to join Lieutenant Scotti and the main force of paratroopers at the bridge which had been held open. Scotti had been amazed to see them return so quickly, thought something must have gone wrong. When Dick Donnelly told him about the blowing up of the two bridges, the lieutenant had looked at the quiet little Slade with admiration.

"I never knew a man whose nickname fitted him less," he said. "He doesn't look like a man called 'Boom-Boom'!"

"Except when he's about to blow up a bridge," Dick replied.

There had been a good battle when the retreating Germans tried to take the bridge back from the paratroopers. But Scotti's forces had been augmented by other parachute companies which had been on other missions, and they succeeded in holding off the Germans until the advancing Americans on the other side had caught up with them. And then the Germans, caught between the two fires, had been annihilated.

Max Burckhardt insisted that this Sicilian action had been the best of all they had taken part in. He had seen more men in the hated Nazi uniform go down under a withering fire, and he had talked to some of the prisoners afterward. They always seemed a little surprised to find a man speaking perfect German, with a family in Germany, fighting against them this way, and Max enjoyed watching their bewilderment, and enjoyed seeing the first doubts creep into their minds about whether or not their Fuehrer really would lead them to victory in this war against the democracies.

After the tough fighting in Sicily, Captain Marker's company of paratroopers—but the Captain was a Major by this time—had been given a three weeks' rest in Algiers. They enjoyed it immensely until they learned that they had missed the landing at Salerno because of their furloughs. But later they were based on the Italian mainland, not far behind the advancing American and British troops fighting their way up the peninsula. When the advance slowed down, became bogged in mud and then stopped by the Germans who entrenched themselves in the hills and fought for every inch of territory, the three-star general went into a huddle with his staff.

"We've got to pull an ace out of our sleeves," he said. "We won't get going until we've taken Maletta, and we're still twenty miles away from it. Yes—we've got to pull a fast one."

"Like the Wadizam Pass action?" an aide suggested.

"Well—not quite," the general said, "but it gives me an idea."

He studied the map of the region around the town of Maletta. It was a small town. More than a village, it was still not a city of any great size or importance, until this moment. There was a junction of two railroads there—and also of the two main roads leading north. Other roads which cut across the many hills were steep and almost impassable for heavily motorized and mechanized forces. The Americans knew they would have to drive straight up the Maletta valley to that town and take it. Then they could really move ahead. Until then they were stuck. And cracking Maletta looked like an almost impossible job because of the peculiarities of the land around it.

"Maybe a variation of the Wadizam technique would work," the general said. "Let's go over the possibilities."

For hours the men planned, checked, threw out one plan and devised another. Three days later they called Major Marker to them and went over the plan with him.

"Just about six men, that's all," the general said. "It sounds like a tiny force to send on this job, but a larger one would be spotted and rounded up. They'd trip over their own feet. But six men—yes, they might be able to do it if they were really good men. After your other successes, Major, we concluded you might have the men under your command."

"Yes, I've got the men," the Major said with a smile. "I'd like to go along myself."

"Can't spare you for this job," the general said. "We need you too much elsewhere."

"What do you need especially?" the Major asked. "What special qualifications must the men have?"

"Well, most of them should speak Italian—and well, too," the general said. "You might have someone who speaks German along, too, because it's Germans we're fighting. The Italians will work with the underground, of course, and they've got to be able to make the underground accept and trust them. Then, among them, you must choose a really good radio man and a demolition expert."

"I'll do it, sir," the Major replied. "I can pick my men without any trouble. And they're men who'll do the job if it can conceivably be done—and maybe they can do it even if it's impossible!"

"Oh—like the gang which came back from the

Major Marker and the Men Went Over Their Plan

dam in the Wadizam Pass action?" the general laughed. "They did the impossible."

"Yes, I'm thinking of some of those same men," Major Marker replied. "Who shall give them their instructions?"

"I'll do it myself," the general said. "Can you have them here tomorrow afternoon?"

"Yes, sir," the Major replied. "Tomorrow afternoon—six picked men."

And so it was that six men set off with Major Marker for the general's headquarters. At first they did not know that was where they were going, but the Major told them after they were speeding along the road in the big command car. Then they were more mystified than ever. The Major would say nothing but, "Something special. Very interesting job. Wish I could go too."

Next to him sat Lieutenant Jerry Scotti, who was to be in command on this mysterious mission. There was Dick Donnelly, second in command, and Corporal Tony Avella for the radio work. Taking up enough room for almost two men in the rear seat was Private Vincent Salamone, the home-run king of baseball in peacetime, the toughest paratrooper of them all in war. As the Major later remarked to the general, "Everybody in Italy knows the name of Vince Salamone. He's an idol over here just the way he is at home. He'll win over the Italians in a minute!"

All those four men spoke Italian well, like natives. They knew Italy and the Italian people thoroughly. Major Marker felt sure that with four out of six speaking Italian so well, this qualification of the general's had been met with complete satisfaction. The fifth man was Private Max Burckhardt. He spoke German, and he was a veteran of the Wadizam dam suicide detachment. The sixth man, since he had to be a demolition expert, was George "Boom-Boom" Slade, who now sat silently beside Vince Salamone, looking most insignificant beside the bulk of the famous ball player.

Major Marker looked over his six selections and smiled. They were all good tough fighters, with plenty of seasoning. And they got along well together. They were good personal friends. The Major knew that Lieutenant Scotti was "Jerry" to the rest of them except when other officers were around. And he knew that the whole crowd would follow Dick Donnelly to the ends of the earth.

The general was impressed too, but not so much as the six men who suddenly found themselves in his presence. Inside of ten minutes, however, they were at their ease. They sat in a plain room with a desk, a big table, about ten chairs, and some large maps on the wall. The general sat at ease, with his collar open, smoking a cigarette. First, he made the men feel at ease when he talked with them about the Wadizam Pass affair and other actions in which they had taken part. He seemed familiar with all details, much to their surprise.

When he saw that they were comfortable and no longer awed, the general plunged into his plan at once.

"The town of Maletta," he said, pointing to the map, "is really our bottleneck. We've still got twenty miles to go to reach it. We can make that twenty miles all right, but taking the town then is a tougher job. It's at the head of a valley up which we'll be fighting to reach it. There are German gun emplacements all along the hills on both sides of the valley. If we follow conventional tactics we can make it—but in about two months. We'll have to clean out all the hills on both sides as we move forward. Oh—we can do it, but at a great cost of time and of men. We'll take that time and use those men if we have to. But I don't think we'll have to."

He paused and looked around at the faces of the men who hung on every word he said. Then he turned to the map again.

"As you can see, we can't by-pass the valley and Maletta itself," he explained. "The country on either side of the valley is rugged and slow going, with bad roads and paths. We can get infantry around there—with machine guns and mortars, but that's about all. And even doing it from both sides, that wouldn't be enough to take Maletta, with the heavy guns the Germans have there."

Lieutenant Scotti nodded his head without realizing it, seeing exactly what the general's problem was.

"Likewise a regular parachute action would be sure to fail," the high officer went on. "Even in great force you'd lack the necessary heavy guns. But six specially equipped paratroopers—they can do a real job for us!"

He smiled at the men and they smiled back. They did not need to say they were eager to take on this job. It showed plainly in their eyes and in their smiles.

"The main job you are to do will come exactly one week from the time you arrive outside Maletta," the general pointed out. "But you must get there in advance and meanwhile do many valuable small jobs for us. You can get detailed information for us on the movement of German troops in and around Maletta—and trucks, tanks, guns, supplies. You see, we'll start our push up the valley at once and we expect the Germans to pour their men into Maletta as a result. Right now they're not sure we plan on taking the road right straight ahead. As soon as they're sure, they'll put just about all they've got into the head of the valley."

The general turned with a pointer and showed them the lines of railroads and roads.

"You can see that Maletta is an important hub, even though it is ordinarily a town of only about ten thousand people. By the way—do any of you men know Maletta?"

Tony Avella raised his hand. "Yes, sir," he said. "I know Maletta pretty well. I've got an uncle who lives there—at least he *did* live there. I haven't heard about him for some time, and he was no great lover of Mussolini."

"Good for him!" said the general. "I hope he's still there. If he is, he may be able to help us greatly. And he certainly can be the go-between in your relations with the Italian townspeople. There aren't ten thousand people there now, by any means, by the way. Most of the civilians have been evacuated. The Germans have made the town into a fortress. And there were no real factories there to keep any sizable part of the population in the town to run them. According to our information there are no more than fifteen hundred Italians left in and around Maletta."

The general came back to the immediate plan for the six men on the special mission.

"We'll want reports, by radio, on troops and supplies into Maletta," he said. "Where you can set up your short-wave radio will be your problem. And how to keep it from being found out by the German detectors is also your problem, I'm afraid, and a tough one. But you'll do it, I'm sure."

Tony shook his head wonderingly. He was glad the general had such confidence in them, but he knew how hard it was to keep a radio station from being located almost immediately when there were detectors listening at all times for underground or enemy stations. Still, they could try! If the general needed it—well, they'd just have to give him what he wanted!

"Finally, you are to be in sufficiently close touch with the townspeople to warn them when you blow up the dam," the general said. "And that's a dangerous job, for there are still some ardent fascists among them, without a doubt, men who are working with the Germans. Not many, I'm sure, but a few. If Corporal Avella's uncle is still there, he'll be able to let you know whom to avoid. But everybody else must be warned—not too soon, but in time, to get to the hills when the dam goes, for the waters will rush down and wipe out Maletta!"

"Oh boy!" Dick Donnelly cried, without thinking. The general grinned at him.

"You seem to like dams, Sergeant Donnelly," he said.

"I like the idea of really blowing one up," Dick replied, "and washing away a few thousand Germans, with their tanks, trucks, guns, and ammunition!"

"Could I ask a question, sir?" Scotti inquired.

"Of course, Lieutenant Scotti," the general answered. "I want you all to ask as many questions about this as you please."

"What about the flood waters when they reach our own troops?" Scotti asked.

"I'll show you," the general replied. "Our men coming up the valley will be here when the dam is blown up." He pointed to a spot on the map about ten miles below the town. "As you see, the valley broadens here. The waters will be pretty low by this time, and they'll channel chiefly into these two river beds, leaving a ridge of high ground up the center between them."

"But how can we attack the town, then?" Jerry asked.

"We won't attack it from the front, up the valley," the general replied. "The flood will have silenced the big guns in the town itself, and for some distance behind it. We'll have infantry pouring over the sides of the hills on both sides at that moment. You'll recall I said we could filter plenty of men up the other sides of these hills, but no heavy guns. Well, with the German guns out of commission, they won't be handicapped. They'll be fighting German foot soldiers on an equal basis, only the Germans will be racing like fury to get into the hills away from the flood waters, and they won't be organized."

"I see, sir," Lieutenant Scotti replied. "I knew there was an answer, of course, but wanted to be sure what it was."

"Naturally," the general replied. "You can see

it's something like the Wadizam Pass action. First comes our advance part way up the valley, drawing heavy German troop and supply movement into Maletta. Meanwhile other forces filter north along the other sides of the ridges, traveling chiefly at night to avoid detection. You men are in Maletta, reporting to us. You warn the Italians, blow up the dam and run for the hills, planning to meet our own men who'll be coming over them at that time."

Then the general asked for questions, and he answered them for half an hour until the six men felt that they knew every detail of the plan, every action that was expected of them.

"One last thing," the general said. "In getting into the town you may find that uniforms are attention-getters. But if you're back of the enemy lines without uniforms you're really spies and can be treated as such by the enemy. In uniform, if captured, you will be prisoners of war. But that problem will have to be left up to you and Lieutenant Scotti, your commanding officer. You do whatever you think is necessary and advisable, but you must be fully aware of the consequences. I have no right to ask you to be spies, to take such a risk. This whole venture is completely volunteer, anyway. Not a man of you needs to undertake it."

But every man *did* want to undertake the job. They were delighted when the general said they would leave the following night. Then, after hearty handshakes and good wishes from the general, the six men left with Major Marker. They jabbered excitedly all the way back to their base, but stopped entirely as soon as they were with their friends in camp. These men all knew that the six were going to do something special, but they could not get the slightest hint of what it was to be. And they were the envy of the whole base. Only "Boom-Boom" Slade seemed unexcited, unperturbed. He was interested chiefly in how much dynamite they'd be able to have, and he spent every spare moment alone studying the plans and photographs of the big dam which had been given him.

"The spillway," he murmured to himself happily. "That looks good for the charge. It ought to be a pretty sight when it goes out!"

The next day was a busy one for most of them. Tony Avella was going over his radio equipment, the very finest short-wave set in the Army. It was put up in special containers for being dropped by parachute, but Tony took them out and practiced setting everything up in a hurry several times. Sergeant Slade was going over his equipment, dynamite, detonator, wires, fuses. Lieutenant Scotti was checking supplies with Dick Donnelly. They took plenty of canned rations, lengths of rope, blinker lights for emergency signaling, extra first-aid kits, blanket beds, waterproof tarpaulins. They tried to think in advance of every condition under which they might have to work, fight, and live.

"We don't want to load ourselves down," Scotti said, "but we want to have everything possible that we'll really be likely to need. One extra supply parachute won't make much difference. We'll set up headquarters in the hills to the east of the town—that's the wildest country thereabouts, and the safest. We might as well make ourselves comfortable for a week's stay, and conduct our forays into the town from the camp base in the hills."

"We might be able to move right into the town," Dick suggested, "if the underground is really helpful and trustworthy."

"Maybe so," the lieutenant agreed. "But that will depend on whether the Germans suspect we're anywhere around. I imagine as soon as Tony gets his radio going, even though our messages will be in code in Italian, they'll suspect something and search the town thoroughly."

"How can we possibly set up the radio so they won't find us?" Dick asked.

"I don't know," Jerry replied with a smile. "That's a really tough assignment. Of course, we plan to go on the air only twice a day and then only for about three or four minutes. Maybe we can move it to a different place each time."

"But we couldn't move it far enough to keep away from them," Dick said. "They'll search the whole area when they get a fix on that short-wave sending set. And we can't have it near our base in the hills, or they'll be right up there after us."

"Yes—it would be best to have it somewhere in the town itself," Scotti said, "though right now I don't see how it's possible. Then the Germans would just think it was an illegal Italian station. They wouldn't necessarily suspect that Americans were there."

"I guess we can't figure that one out until we get there," Dick concluded.

"No, that will have to wait," the lieutenant agreed. "And how we'll manage to blow up that dam I don't know. It must be pretty well guarded."

"Boom-Boom Slade can figure out something, I'll bet," Dick said. "That guy can manage to blow up anything if you really want it blown up!"

At nine o'clock that evening everything was ready. The six men reported to Major Marker, who took them at once to the big car. Without lights they drove over the roads of southern Italy for an hour, eventually reaching a small airfield. They had no idea where they might be, as they had gone through no towns.

On the field, a big transport waited in the darkness, its two engines idling. First, the equipment was placed in the plane, and then the men climbed aboard. Before the door closed, Scotti and Dick Donnelly waved a last farewell to Major Marker, who seemed no more than a shadow on the ground below.

"Happy landings!" came his voice over the sound of the motors, and then they closed the door. Scotti nodded to the pilot in the cockpit and the plane picked up speed. In a minute more its wheels had left the ground and they were in the air, on their way to the most dangerous undertaking any of them had ever faced.

CHAPTER SEVEN

NOT SO HAPPY LANDINGS

It was a short trip. Their base was not far behind the front lines below Maletta, and the field to which they had gone was only a few miles further south and—they guessed—some distance to the east.

"The Air Forces are sending up some bombers for a little diversion," Scotti said to the men around him. "They'll pull the German fighter strength and ack-ack fire to the railroad bridges northwest of the town. And they'll fill the air with plenty of sound for the German sound detectors, so that they're likely to miss the sound of our plane. We'll fly low so that the plane can't easily be seen above the hills beyond us."

"Never landed at night before," Dick Donnelly said, "except on flat desert land."

"It's tricky, all right," Scotti said, "when there are hills and trees below. And there's no moon to see by tonight. That's good from one angle because we can't be seen easily either. But you can't tell where you're coming down. Maybe some of us will spend the night caught in some treetops."

Tony Avella shrugged his shoulders. "It's all in the game," he said. "We'll make out all right."

The others nodded without speaking, and there was silence in the plane. Five minutes passed this way before the co-pilot stepped back to say quietly, "This is it."

The men stood up at once, and the fuselage door was thrown open. Tony Avella and Dick Donnelly heaved out the two parachutes carrying the radio equipment, and Tony followed immediately, as if he could not be parted from them for more than a few seconds.

"Go ahead, Dick," Scotti said, and the sergeant leaped without a word. Then the lieutenant helped Slade and Vince Salamone throw out the four parachutes bearing the containers of dynamite and demolition equipment.

"Right after it, Slade," Scotti said. "Each man finds his own stuff. Vince will find you and help you with it."

Little Slade closed his eyes and his face was pale. It still seemed almost to kill him to make a parachute leap but he never said a word about it. He was hardly out the door when the huge bulk of Salamone went after him.

Now only Max Burckhardt and Scotti were left. Together they tossed out the three remaining supply parachutes.

"See you later, Max," the lieutenant said. "Everybody will head east toward me, you know. But we may not get together until daylight."

With a grin, Max jumped. Scotti turned and waved to the plane's co-pilot, then stepped into space shouting "Geronimo!" It always seemed a little strange to him to call out his own first name when he jumped. But he didn't smile about it tonight. Jumping in the darkness was no light-hearted task, and the week ahead of them was filled with responsibilities such as he had never shouldered before.

"Most of the others are down by now," he said to himself. "Hope they're not in trouble."

He tried to look below, but there was nothing but blackness, just a little blacker than the sky around him. In the skies to the northwest he saw the bursts of antiaircraft fire from the German batteries, trying to find the American bombers that were coming over the railroad tracks. Searchlights stabbed the sky, cutting sharp white lines in the blackness, and Scotti was glad, despite his wish for a little light, that they were not searching for him.

Tony Avella was on the ground already. He, who seemed worried the least about landing on a wooded hillside at night, had no trouble at all. He came down in a little clearing, hit the ground with a hard jolt because he was not expecting it quite so soon, and rolled down the slope about ten feet. His 'chute had collapsed of its own accord and he slipped out of the harness quickly. Then he set about trying in the darkness to find his two containers of radio

Jumping in the Darkness Was No Lighthearted Task

material.

"Probably can't locate a thing at night," he muttered to himself, "but think of the time I can save if I find even one of them. Dick was right behind me. Wonder if he made out okay."

Dick Donnelly did not have the luck of Tony. At that moment he was hanging head down in a tree. One leg was over a heavy branch, and his 'chute shroud lines were caught far above. His face and hands were badly scratched by the branches as he had plunged into them, but he was not worried about such minor trifles. He was struggling to pull himself up to a sitting position on the branch. Every time he tried, his shroud lines seemed to tug him in the other direction. Finally, however, he succeeded in getting the other leg over the branch. Then he snaked his pocket knife from his trousers and reached back to cut the shroud lines which held him.

When he had cut through four of them, he felt the pull lessen and found he could pull himself up on the branch. For a few moments he sat there, waiting for his head to stop swimming as the blood receded from it. Finally, he cut the rest of his parachute lines and was free.

"Can't leave that 'chute up there," he said. "It might be spotted from below in the morning, and certainly a German plane would see it before long."

Tug as he might, however, he could not get it

free. Making up his mind that he'd have to free it by the first light of dawn, he felt for the tree trunk, found it, and began to let himself down. His eyes were more accustomed to the darkness now, and he could vaguely see the branches as he stepped down from one to the other. Then the ground loomed up about ten feet below, and he let himself drop. He rolled over once, then brought himself up to a sitting position.

"Now what?" he asked himself. "Just sit here, I guess. If I leave this tree I may get lost and not find it again to get that parachute."

So he edged his way back a couple of feet until his back rested against the trunk of the tree in which he had fallen. He moved a rock beneath one leg, and then relaxed completely, his head back against the tree. Far off he heard the roaring thud of bombs dropped by American bombers, and he smiled.

"Wish I could locate Tony," he said to himself. "We went out so close together he can't be far away. Hm—that reminds me—Tony asked if sometime when we were out alone at night I wouldn't sing *Celeste Aïda* for him. Well, I'd do it if he were here now. But it's been so long since I've sung. Haven't even thought much about singing."

Hardly realizing what he was doing he began to hum aloud the slow, ascending first notes of the famous tenor aria from the Verdi opera. By the time he reached the third phrase, he was singing the words, and it felt good. It still sounded all right. He kept on, letting his voice out more and more, pulling himself to his feet finally so that he could sing in full voice. Only when he had come to the end, did he realize that he had perhaps done a foolish thing, singing so loudly there in the hills behind the enemy lines.

Then he heard a soft clapping of hands and the word "Bravo!" He jumped and looked into the darkness from which the sound came. "Bravo, Ricardo Donnelli!" the voice said again, and Dick knew who it was as he made out the advancing figure.

"Tony!" he cried. "You startled me!"

"Sorry," the radioman said, as he came close. "But that's nothing to what you would have done to any German soldier within half a mile!"

"I know—I didn't realize," Dick said. "I got to humming when I remembered you wanted me to sing it for you sometime when we were alone in the hills at night. And then, first thing I knew, I was really singing it."

"I was kidding," Tony said. "In the first place I'm quite sure there isn't a German within half a mile. And if there were, he'd just think it was an Italian out singing in the night. You didn't sound at all like the German idea of an American soldier. You sounded swell, incidentally. I could close my eyes and see the whole scene on the stage at the

Met."

"Well, we're a long way from there," Dick said. "And I'm a long way from doing any singing again."

"Gee, I was just thinking," Tony said. "In Maletta, they used to have a pretty fair little opera company. Maybe it's not going now, though the Italians have kept up their opera performances under the worst conditions. That's about the last thing they'll give up. Wouldn't this Maletta Opera group love to have you as a guest star for a performance or two!"

"Yes, and the Germans would applaud vigorously, too, I'll bet," Dick laughed. "How'd you make out in your landing, by the way?"

"Neat!" Tony replied. "Right in a clearing. I went crawling around looking for my radio but couldn't find anything. Then I heard you singing and came this way."

"I wound up head down in this tree here," Dick said. "Had to cut myself out of my 'chute. Couldn't get it out of the tree, though. I'll have to do it when it first gets light. No use waving a signal flag like that at the Germans to let them know we're here."

"Well, we can't do anything until it does get light," Tony said. "So let's sit down."

They sat on the ground and leaned against the trunk of the tree. Then they talked for a while, as the sound of bombing and antiaircraft fire northwest of Maletta died out. Finally they both fell into a light sleep.

It was still dark when Dick woke up, but not as black as it had been when they landed the night before. Somewhere to the east, the first rays of the sun were climbing the hills, and a hazy grayness was the first notice of their advance. Dick realized that his neck was so stiff he could hardly turn it, and then he knew that one foot was asleep.

"Dick—awake?" It was Tony's voice beside him.

"Sure—just woke up," Dick replied. "But I don't know if I can move. My neck feels as if it would snap in two if I tried to turn it."

"Same here," Tony said. "But I think it's going to begin getting light before long. We might be able to get something done."

"I know it," Dick agreed. "The Germans might have planes going over pretty early and I don't want them to spot any 'chutes."

With an effort he got to his feet, wagging his head from side to side while he grimaced with the pain. Then he stamped his sleeping foot on the hard earth while it tingled to life. He turned and looked at Tony Avella, who was going through the same thing.

"Do I look as groggy as you do, Tony?" he laughed.

"If you look as groggy as I feel," Tony answered, "you're pretty bad. I can't see without a fuzziness over everything."

But in a few minutes they were awake. Together

they scrambled up the big tree and got Dick's parachute untangled from the branches. Wrapping it up in a bundle with the harness, Dick slung it over his shoulder.

"Don't want to leave any evidence like this around," he said, following Tony off through the trees to help him find his things.

Tony's 'chute was only about fifty yards from the tree in which Dick had landed. They stowed the two parachutes together and then walked south searching for the two radio 'chutes. They found the first one almost at once. It was caught on an overhanging rock over a sheer drop of about thirty feet to a stone ledge below.

"Glad I didn't land there," Tony commented, as he crawled up the rock to the 'chute. There he tugged the shroud lines so that the container, which was hanging free in the air, swung over close to Dick, who caught it and cut it loose. Then Tony retrieved the colored 'chute and they continued the search for the other one.

It took them ten minutes to find it, and by that time dawn had really come. The birds in the trees were chirping and flitting about but no other sound came to them. When they had gathered everything together, they set out to find the others of their party.

"Must be about three-quarters of a mile," Dick said. "No matter how fast they went out of the ship they'd be spread over that much territory. We can start whistling pretty soon."

After a hundred steps through the trees, heading northward parallel with the ridge of the hill above them, they began alternately to give poor imitations of bird calls. But the birds themselves were singing so vigorously, as if they did not realize a war was going on, that the two Americans began to wonder if their calls would be heard. In a few minutes, however, they heard a call like their own.

"That's no bird," Tony said. "Only Vince Salamone could make a sound like that."

They hurried down to the left, from which the whistle had come, lugging their heavy containers with them. They saw Vince Salamone and "Boom-Boom" Slade sitting on their equipment under a tree. Vince was working so hard at whistling that he could not hear the replies which Dick and Tony were giving him. And Slade was pursing up his lips repeatedly without a single sound coming out. The demolition expert could not whistle a note!

Dick called out when they were close, and the two men jumped to their feet. Happy to learn that neither one had been hurt in his landing, Dick checked over the equipment to be sure it was all there.

"Right—three containers and five 'chutes!" he said. "Let's go."

Dick led the way as they went forward to the north again. It was hard walking, for the hill was steeper, and ahead Dick could make out an outcropping of rock that rose straight up for about twenty-five feet. He began to whistle once more, looking for either Max Burckhardt or Jerry Scotti. After a few minutes he heard an answering whistle and stopped.

"Where's that coming from?" Dick asked, puzzled. The whistle seemed to be ahead of them, but just where was not certain. So they walked forward more steps, whistled again, and heard a reply. Then they heard a voice.

"Dick! Dick! I'm up here!"

They all looked up. There, leaning over a rocky ledge far above them, was Max Burckhardt.

"Max! How did you get up there?" Dick called back, not too loudly.

"How do you think?" Max demanded angrily. "I landed here, of course!"

"On that little ledge?" Tony asked. "How big is it?"

"About eight feet square," Max replied. "And there's not a way to get off it. Sheer rock up above and straight drop below. Not a foothold anywhere. I feel silly as the devil perched up here with no way to get down."

"You may feel silly," Dick answered, "but you're really lucky as the devil. You might have been knocked senseless against this cliff by your 'chute."

"Don't I know it!" Max called back.

"Where's your 'chute?" Dick asked.

"Here!" Max replied. "I sort of sensed I was on the edge of something and I pulled it in fast. It was trying to pull me right off. Toss me up a good rope. There's a rock up here I can fasten it on."

Dick quickly opened one of the supply containers and found a good length of rope. It took half a dozen tries to get one end of it up to Max, but soon he had it looped over the rock. He tossed one end down again.

"With both ends down there," he explained, "we can get it free from this jutting rock and take it along with us. Hold it taut for me and it won't come loose."

Max tossed his 'chute over to them, and then Dick and Vince Salamone bore down on the ends of the rope. Soon Max slid over the edge and came hand-over-hand down to the ground.

"Boy, am I glad to see you guys!" he exclaimed. "I was beginning to feel that I'd be up there for the duration."

Gathering everything together again, they went in search of the other supply containers and within another ten minutes had found them intact.

"Now to find Jerry," Dick said. "He can't be far."

"I know it," Max said. "I've been wondering. I would have thought he might come back a bit looking for me, and I certainly think he would have looked around for the last supply 'chutes. He was jumping right after them."

They stopped and whistled. There was no answer. Then they moved forward a short distance and whistled again. Still no reply came to them. Dick climbed up the hill a little farther and called out to the others. He had found the entrance to a cave. It was well sheltered and not very obvious, and inside it was like a large square room. But they found no Lieutenant Scotti inside, nor any sign that a human had been in the place for a long time.

"This will make a swell base," Dick said, "as soon as we find Jerry. Let's stow all our stuff here and fan out to look for him."

Quickly they put their supplies and equipment well back in the dry cave and then started out in different directions from the cave entrance. It was Dick who first heard the groan, coming from behind a huge, jagged boulder. He raced around it quickly, whistling the signal frantically as he went.

There at the bottom of the boulder lay Lieutenant Scotti. His face was covered with blood, and his right leg was twisted under him in a way that told Dick immediately that it was broken.

CHAPTER EIGHT

TWO VISITORS TO TOWN

The others came running to the boulder in a moment. Dick had felt the Lieutenant's pulse and found it still strong. The blood on his face was from two deep gashes in his skull, obviously from the jagged rock against which he had fallen.

Vince Salamone picked up the lieutenant in his arms and carried him gently up the hill to the cave. Tony and Max ran ahead to get out some of the blanket beds from the supply containers, and finally Scotti was resting inside the cave.

"Tony and Max," Dick said, "see if you can find water. There ought to be some little stream or springs near by in hills like this."

The two men snatched up canteens and went out quickly. Meanwhile, Dick looked over Scotti's broken leg. Salamone looked on as if he wished he could do something. Slade, who had said almost nothing, came to Dick's side.

"I happen to know a little bit about such things," he said, almost timidly. "Let me have a look."

Deftly he ripped away the lieutenant's trouser leg and examined the break in the bone, just a little above the knee.

"Seems to be pretty clean," he said. "We'll have to get it set right away. Need some long straight pieces of wood."

"I'll get 'em," Vince said, happy that there was something he could do to help. He pulled a hatchet from the supply container, made sure his knife was in his pocket, and went out of the cave.

In a moment Max and Tony both returned with water and Slade bathed Scotti's face and his wounds. Opening a first-aid kit, he put a little sulfa powder in the deep wounds and then dressed them.

"He's completely unconscious as a result of these," he said to Dick. "Can't tell if there's any concussion of the brain or not, of course. If there is, it's bad, and he may not come to. But if not he'll come around. We mustn't try to force him back to consciousness, though. Just make him comfortable and let him rest."

Dick nodded in agreement and the little demolition expert, who now turned out to be also a first-aid expert, went quickly over the rest of Scotti's body to see if there were any more wounds. He found nothing but some torn flesh on one hand, where he had probably tried to clutch at the rock when he landed on it. Slade quickly cleaned and dressed this wound, too, felt the lieutenant's pulse, and stepped back.

"Can't do anything else except set the leg," he said.

Max and Tony had gone to help Vince find the straight pieces of wood needed for this task. In a few minutes they returned with straight sapling trunks about an inch and a half in diameter, but Slade said the wood was too pliable.

"That could never hold a broken leg in position," he said. "It would bend with the leg. You've got to find old wood, hard and stiff."

The three men went off into the woods again, and soon Dick could hear the sound of a hatchet chopping wood. He hoped that the sound did not carry to the town below, or to any German garrison which might be near by. The town was about two miles away, and the main German gun emplacements on the hills were a good way to the south of them, but still Dick did not rest easy until the sound was ended.

In ten minutes the three men returned with wood that Slade declared perfect. It was straight and true, with all tiny branches cleaned off smoothly, and there was no give in it at all. Slade set the others to tearing one of the parachutes into strips, and these strips he tied around the two long pieces of wood which were placed on either side of Scotti's broken leg.

In twenty minutes the job was done.

"Best I can do, anyway," Slade said. "Maybe it will set all right and maybe not. Nothing else to do, though. The main thing I'm worried about is the

Slade Set Scotti's Broken Leg

head injury."

"Yes, I wish he weren't unconscious," Dick said. "It seems terrible, somehow, to see him here but not talk to him, hear him. And right now we need him badly. He's the one with the brains in this outfit."

"It's too bad, all right," Tony said, "but you've got a pretty good head on your shoulders, too, Dick. We can carry on. And, anyway, maybe Scotti will come around in a little while and he can direct operations from here. He doesn't have to move around. We can do everything that needs to be done."

The others agreed, but Dick felt a little lost without Scotti's help at this point. He set about getting the cave organized, the containers unpacked, the supplies in order. Tony Avella checked over all the radio material and found everything in order.

Slade stacked his dynamite at the rear of the cave, and Vince said, as he saw the great pile, "Are you just going to blow up *one* dam with that, Boom-Boom? It looks as if you had enough for two."

"It takes a lot of dynamite to blow up a good dam," Slade said. "From the pictures and plans I saw, this isn't such a wonderful one. Structurally, it would never be acceptable in the United States. But, when possible, I always believe in bringing along just twice as much material as I think I'm going to need."

"And who knows?" Tony laughed. "Maybe we can find something else we can blow up with whatever's left over."

"Not a bad idea," Dick said. "Not a bad idea at all."

They all sat down at the mouth of the cave and opened their cans of rations. Dick said he thought it was all right to light a small fire for a short while so they might have coffee. In five minutes there were five cups being held over a little blaze, and soon the coffee was made. The men all drank it with relish and sighs of relief, and then the fire was put out.

"Nobody'll spot that little bit of smoke and get suspicious," Max said.

"We just shouldn't do it too often," Dick said. "If they should notice it regularly, they'd come to investigate."

Every half hour, at least, Dick went to Scotti's side, felt his pulse, and looked eagerly for some signs of consciousness. But the lieutenant remained in the same state, breathing shallowly, but with a good pulse beat.

By four o'clock in the afternoon, Dick felt sure that whatever decisions were made that day would have to come from him. Vince and Max had taken short naps, but now they were awake and asking him what the plan of action was. He called them all around him to talk the matter over.

"We can't do much of anything except at night, of course," Dick said. "And we haven't got much time to waste. First, we've got to get the radio set up, somehow, somewhere. Any ideas, Tony?"

"Not up here," Tony said. "That's about all I can say now, Dick. They'd spot us in no time with their detectors, and we'd have a company of Germans all over the side of this hill."

"Where, then?" Dick asked.

"In the town itself," Tony replied.

"That seems next to impossible, Tony," Max said. "Why, they'll find it in a minute in town—even if you should find some way to get all that paraphernalia in without being caught."

"I know it sounds out of the question," Tony agreed. "But there must be some place we can set it up without being located. Now, if my uncle's still around—"

"How are you going to find that out?" Vince asked.

"Go to town and ask," Tony replied. "Isn't that right, Dick?"

"Yes, that's right," Dick replied. "I don't know about getting the radio into town, but we've got to go down there, some of us, and find out what's what. That uncle of yours, Tony—we might as well assume he's *not* there. So many people have been evacuated. What did he do there, anyway?"

"That's one reason I think he might still be there," Tony said. "For quite a few years, he's been caretaker at the Villa Rolta. Right on the edge of town, the villa is—a big place about a thousand years old, backing up against the steep hill at the northern end of town. Belonged to the Rolta family ever since the twelfth century, though none of them have been around for quite a while. It's been sort of a Museum for a long time now, and Uncle Tomaso has been caretaker. He's an old duck and I don't think he'd move. He'd stick there at the villa no matter what happened."

"Well, maybe so," Dick said. "It would be lucky if he were still around. We've got to find that out. And we've got to make contact with somebody else there if he isn't around. That's a ticklish job. The first man we talk to might be a friend of the Germans."

"We'll just listen first," Tony said. "You can tell, after a little while, by the way people talk."

"But what kind of listening can a bunch of American soldiers in uniform do?" Vince asked.

"That brings up another point," Dick said. "You all remember what the General said about that. If we got out of uniform and were caught we'd be treated as spies. And you know that means getting shot—right away and without any questions asked."

"Sure, but we can't go in uniform," Tony protested.

"I don't think we can, either," Dick said. "And I know Scotti didn't think so. That's why he got hold of six sets of clothing, clothing of ordinary Italian small-town people such as they'd be wearing in Maletta these days."

"Do they fit?" demanded Vince Salamone, whose difficulty in finding clothes large enough was always bothering him.

Dick laughed. "Yes, Jerry did a good job on that," he said. "Of course, it was pretty easy to pick up the right things fast in the towns we've recently taken over in southern Italy. He even found a couple of Italians as big as you, Vince."

"Then we go in Italian clothes?" Tony asked.

"Only if you want to," Dick replied. "I'm not going to ask anybody to do it who doesn't agree perfectly with the idea. But I know that I'm going to leave my uniform here in the cave when I visit Maletta."

"Same here," Tony said. "I'll be right at home. Nobody'll ever notice me. And if they ask, I'm just little Antonio Avella, from the town of Carlini up north, come down looking for my poor old uncle."

"What kind of Italian peasant do you think I'll make?" Max asked. "I can't speak the language."

"You're my deaf and dumb cousin!" Tony laughed, and the others joined in. "I always knew part of that was true, but now you'll have to fill the description completely."

"Okay," Max laughed. "I'll be deaf and dumb if it means I can help and at the same time keep from getting myself shot as a spy."

"Maybe we can pick up a German uniform for you," Dick said, "and then your German will come in mighty handy. Come to think of it, I'm going to keep on the lookout for a spare uniform."

"Make me a high officer, if you get me a German uniform," Max said. "I'd like to be more than a private for a while, especially if I've got to wear a Nazi uniform. It would be fun to get in a Colonel's uniform and march up to a company of soldiers and order them to jump in the lake and drown themselves. They'd do it, too! They're just that crazy about obeying orders if the orders are barked by a guy with enough gold braid on him."

"But I don't speak German or Italian, either one," Slade said. "What about me?"

"Boom-Boom, you stay right here," Dick said. "In the first place, you came along to blow up a dam. You can also be mighty useful by nursing our lieutenant back to life and health. Somebody's got to keep on tap here, anyway, all the time. You're elected."

"All right," Slade said. "But I must have a chance to look over that dam once or twice before I go to blow it up."

"We'll visit the dam, all right," Dick said. "But that will come later. Now here's the schedule, and for most of you guys it's easy."

They all looked at the young sergeant expectantly.

"If too many strange Italians from the north, including a deaf and dumb one, land in this town all of a sudden, some folks will be suspicious. So this first night Tony and I go down to the town to look for his uncle Tomaso or find out whatever we can. Depending on what we learn—we'll lay our plans then."

"And the rest of us just sit here?" Vince demanded.

"Yes, you just sit here," Dick said. "Tony and I will leave as soon as it grows dark. If we don't come back by two a.m. Vince and Max are to come looking for us. Clear?"

They all nodded in agreement. Then Dick went in for another look at Lieutenant Scotti, followed by Slade.

"Isn't there really anything we can do, Boom-Boom?" he asked uneasily.

"Not a thing, sergeant," Slade replied. "I'll confess I'm worried about the lieutenant, but there's nothing we can do. Anything we might try would prove more dangerous than doing nothing at all now."

Dick shook his head and went back to get the Italian peasant clothes. He tossed the sets of clothing to each man according to his size, and then stripped off his uniform and put on the trousers and shirt which Scotti had bought from an Italian many miles to the south.

"If the guy that owned these knew how they were being used," Tony said, as he got into his things, "I'll bet he'd be mighty happy. When this is over I want to look him up and tell him that his clothes helped in the big defeat of the Germans at Maletta."

They ate a meal from their ration cans then, and watched the sun sink over the ridge of hills to the west. By seven o'clock it was completely dark, and Dick Donnelly—once more using the name of Ricardo Donnelli—and Tony Avella started down the hill to visit the town of Maletta.

CHAPTER NINE

UNCLE TOMASO

The two men did not talk for some time as they walked slowly through the dark woods. As the trees began to thin out near the bottom of the hill, Dick thought more carefully about the details of their plan. As they approached the town more closely, it seemed almost impossible to carry such an undertaking through successfully. Here they were walking right into the heart of the enemy's territory, into one of his most important bases.

"We haven't got any identification papers," he said casually to Tony.

"Neither have a great many Italian peasants," Tony replied, "especially if they come from the farms. Either they haven't been given such papers at all, haven't been checked up on, or they forget to carry them. They're like that, you know—not like the Germans at all, who must always have everything so well systematized. The Italian farmer knows that he is Guiseppi Amato, and all his friends know it. Why, he asks, should he bother to carry around a paper saying that's who he is?"

Dick laughed lightly. "And he's right, too," he agreed. "Mussolini really couldn't get very far with his system and rigid discipline and such, cataloguing everybody and everything."

"Of course, the Germans are very contemptuous of the Italians," Tony said, "which is a compliment to the Italians. They don't realize that half of the Italians' apparent carelessness is really a subtle form of opposition. They just forget their identification papers, that's all. And they tell that to the German sentry or officer with the most innocent face, with a sort of helpless shrug of the shoulders. It exasperates the German, of course, but what can he do about it? If only an occasional Italian acted that way, the Germans could shoot him or throw him in a concentration camp as punishment and as an example to the others. But when half the people do it—well!"

"Then if we're asked for papers, we've just forgotten them, or lost them some time ago," Dick concluded.

"Or we don't even seem to know what they're talking about," Tony said. "We're dumb. We're as stupid as the Germans think we are. In that, we're safe."

"But it's a good idea to avoid any more contact with the Germans than we are forced into," Dick said.

"I think so, too, Dick," Tony said. "So I think we ought not to go into Maletta on the main road. They're likely to have sentries posted on the main roads into town, just to check on people coming and going. We can cross the main road, go through the fields, and cut around to one of the little side streets."

"Good," Dick agreed. "The land is leveling out below us a bit. Looks like a farm."

"Yes, see the lights over there," Tony pointed out. "Farmhouse on our right. If we keep straight ahead across the field now we ought to strike the main road. We can cross it, then circle around to the left toward town, under the shadow of the hill."

"Will that bring us anywhere near the villa where your uncle was caretaker?" Dick asked.

"Yes, right there," Tony replied. "You see that steep hill ahead? You can make out the dark outlines of it against the sky. It's at the foot of that—the villa, backed right up against the hill, almost built into it."

They were walking across the farmer's field now, stepping between the rows of plants. Dick could not make out what they were, but he was careful to avoid stepping on them. Finally they came to a low stone wall marking the end of the field. Beyond it was a ditch and the road. They crouched low beside the fence and listened. Far off a dog barked and from somewhere else another answered him. To the left they could see the lights of Maletta, though there were not many, and no glow was cast in the sky as it would have been in normal times.

The Two Men Walked Toward the Villa

"Okay, let's go across," Dick said, vaulting over the wall.

Tony followed him, and they clambered up the side of the ditch onto the road. It was wide and paved, obviously the main road to the northeast.

"There's another road like this going northwest," Tony said. "Two valleys meet here at Maletta and join into one up which our forces are coming. They form the letter Y, with Maletta at the point where the three arms meet. I imagine most of the German troops and supplies come down to Maletta along the left upper arm of the Y, from the northwest, though some come along this road, which is the right branch of the Y."

"The dam is up to the east a bit, isn't it?" Dick said. "On the right arm of the Y."

"That's right," Tony said. "This road skirts around the edge of the dam and lake, then dips down into the valley. It will be wiped out completely by the flood waters when the dam is blown up."

They were across the road by this time, leaping over another wall into another field.

"Then the waters will pour down through Maletta and into the valley leading to the south, where our main attack seems to be," Dick figured out.

"Yep, and a good flood it will be," Tony said.

"But that leaves the main supply road into Maletta free," Dick said. "The left arm of the Y, leading to the northwest."

"Yes, it does," Tony replied. "But we'll catch plenty of German troops and supplies in Maletta itself, and below it, where they are going to meet our attack."

"But they can escape up the northwest road," Dick said. "We ought to be able to do something about that."

"You want to make it a hundred per cent catastrophe, don't you?" Tony asked with a laugh.

"I surely do," Dick said. "And if we get time, we might take a little walk up that northwest road to look it over."

"Tonight?" Tony asked.

"No, not tonight," was the reply. "Before anything else is done we've got to get your radio set. We're not far from that hill now, are we?"

"No, it's just ahead," Tony said. "We'll head a bit to the left here."

They changed their direction, crawled over another wall, skirted around another house where a barking dog was too curious about them. Then they found themselves on a narrow street with a few small houses on both sides. In one of them a lamp was burning, but the others were dark. It was silent on the street, but Dick and Tony heard the sound of trucks and cars from the center of town ahead of them.

They came to a corner where another street

crossed the one they were on. Tony touched Dick's arm, and they took a right turn. There were a few more houses, then they stopped. The road began to ascend a hill, and then it ended, becoming nothing but a wide path. Tony stopped Dick.

"See, there to the left," he pointed out. "The villa."

Dick looked and saw a huge dark mass. At the front of it there were many lights, and he could see cars standing before the door.

"It seems to be a busy place," he said.

"Yes, it does," Tony agreed. "The Germans must be using it for something."

"Think we'd better try to get there?" Dick wondered.

"Around to the rear, yes," Tony said. "There was a servants' wing at the back on this side, almost cut into the hill. Come on, let's go."

They walked toward the villa along the steep slope of the hill, and Dick saw that they were approaching it from the rear on the east side. They would not be seen by anyone at the front of the building.

They walked slowly now. Dick saw the shape of the building more clearly as they came near it. It was a huge place, built a short way up the hill so that it overlooked the rest of the town spread out below it. He made out what looked like a tall tower rising from the center of it. And then he saw what

Tony must have meant as the servants' wing. It was built right up against the steep hill.

"You could almost come down the hill onto the roof of that wing," he whispered to Tony.

"That's exactly what you *can* do," Tony said. "I've run and jumped onto it when I was over here visiting. I spent most of my time up in Carlini where most of my relatives lived, but I spent a month with Uncle Tomaso here in Maletta."

"That's surely lucky for us," Dick said. "It would be tough without your knowledge of the town."

"If Uncle Tomaso is still around," Tony said, "he'd be in this servants' wing. But of course, if the Germans have taken it over there may be soldiers quartered in there."

"I see a light from the room at the end," Dick said. "Maybe we can look in the window."

Carefully they walked toward the lighted window at the end of the wing, trying not to dislodge the rocks beneath their feet. When they were ten feet away, they went down on all fours and crawled forward. They reached the rough stone wall and edged toward the window.

With one quick motion upward, Dick took one glance through the window, then ducked down again.

"What? What did you see?" Tony asked.

"No German soldiers," Dick said. "Just one old man."

Tony's heart leaped at these words. "Just one old man in my Uncle Tomaso's old room. That must be my uncle—it's just *got* to be!"

"Take a quick look, Tony," Dick said. "Go ahead."

He moved back a bit so that Tony could get near the window. He took a quick glance around to see that no one was approaching. Then he watched Tony's face to see if he could tell by the expression who it was he saw.

Tony moved his head up and looked in the window. He started to bring it down again, but then left it there, looking steadily inside the room. Dick heard his breath come fast. The light from the room fell faintly on his face, and Dick, studying it closely, saw the mouth twitch, the eyes fill with tears. And then Tony spoke, almost in a whisper.

"Uncle Tomaso," he breathed. "My own Uncle Tomaso!"

Then he crouched down beside Dick again. The sergeant said nothing, and Tony could not speak for a few seconds.

"Yes, Dick, it's my uncle," Tony said. "And—he looks so old, sitting there just staring at the floor. He looks sad and broken and old. I almost didn't recognize him."

"Nobody else in the room?" Dick asked.

"No, he's alone," Tony said. "I'll try tapping on the window."

Tony stood up, looked all around, then tapped lightly against the window pane. Dick stood behind him, looking in over Tony's shoulder.

The old man hardly seemed to hear anything at first. He lifted his head slowly as if he might be dreaming. Then suddenly he jumped, startled, and Dick saw fear leap into his eyes. He stared at the door, and went to open it. Then Tony tapped more insistently. Obviously the old man could not be sure where the sound was coming from.

Finally he turned and stared at the window. Tony pressed his face close against the glass so that his uncle might see him, might recognize him. He hated to see that look of fear in Tomaso's face, and he wanted to reassure him quickly.

But the old man looked more terrified than ever. For a few seconds he just stared at the window, not moving, and then as if impelled against his will, he moved toward the window. He moved his arms forward and opened it. Then he spoke, in a small voice, in Italian.

"What—what do you want?"

"Uncle Tomaso!" Tony whispered urgently. "It's me—Tony! Tony Avella! Your nephew from America!"

The old man's eyes widened with unbelief, but he leaned forward, thrusting his face close to Tony's.

"It can't be!" he muttered. "No, I'm dreaming! It can't be! The Americans have not come yet!"

"But I've come, Uncle Tomaso," Tony insisted. "I've come with my friends ahead of the rest of the Americans. Yes, I'm really Tony. Look! Look closely."

The old man did look closely. He stretched one hand through the window and touched Tony's face. Then he began to smile, and his eyes began to shine.

"Tony, my little Tony!" he cried.

"Quiet, Uncle," Tony warned. "Don't bring the Germans here!"

"The Germans!" And Tony's uncle cursed. "The Germans! Soon they will taste some of their own medicine. Are the Americans really so close, Tony, that you could come to me here?"

"Yes, Uncle, and they will be here in another week," Tony said. "But you can help us. Where can we talk?"

"I'll come outside with you," the old man said. "Yes, through the window. I can still crawl through the window."

"Will the Germans come and look in your room?" Tony asked. "Are they likely to miss you?"

"No, they never look for the old man," Tomaso said. "They never even think about the harmless old man, except when they want their rooms cleaned or their boots polished."

Suddenly the old man laughed. "Harmless old man, they think! If they knew what I've done!"

He no longer seemed to be the broken and tired

soul that he was before. He stuck one leg out the open window and climbed through with an agility that surprised Dick. Tony helped him to the ground, and then closed the window almost shut behind him. Then the uncle looked questioningly at Dick.

"Uncle, this is my friend, my commander," Tony explained. "He is really Italian, too, but I call him Dick Donnelly. Uncle—I'll tell you right away who he really is. Ricardo Donnelli!"

"You—you are really Ricardo Donnelli?" the old man exclaimed. "Here in our little town of Maletta?"

Dick smiled and nodded. "But I'm really just a soldier in the American Army now," he said. "We should get away from the villa before we talk. Can we go back up the hill?"

"Yes, back up the hill," the old man said, starting off at once. "It is steep but we can go up there and talk safely. Not far. We cannot be seen up here from the villa."

Dick and Tony followed him up the slope to a little clump of trees.

"This used to be a pleasant place to sit on a sunny afternoon," the old man said. "See—there is a long flat rock to sit upon. Now, I do not come here often, because all I can see are the hated Germans!"

Then he began to pour out a stream of questions to Tony—about his mother and father, how long he had been in the Army, when he had come to

Italy, how far away the American troops were. Then suddenly he stopped.

"You said I could help the Americans," he said. "Tell me what I can do. I shall do anything you ask. And there are many others here who will help. We have not been idle."

"I imagine not," Dick said. "In America we don't hear much about the underground activities in Italy, but we know you have been fighting in every way possible."

"Especially now that there is some hope," Tomaso said. "For so long, for so many many years, we were held under the thumb of that bellowing jackass, Mussolini, with his cruel blackshirt terrorists. And the world did not seem to care. But now—now we know we will be free men again, and we fight once more."

"What can you do, Uncle?" Tony asked.

"Oh, there are a few things an old man can do," Tomaso smiled. "When that big Gestapo chief came here on inspection, it was I who got word to the others who he was. Perhaps you have not heard about the bomb that blew up his car as it drove away—killing him. No? Well, we did that."

Tony and Dick looked at the old man in admiration. Then he went on.

"The power plant at the dam has been damaged half a dozen times. Of course, they could always fix it again, but it delayed them for several days, some-

The Old Man Told of the Underground's Activities

times a week. And they've had to post a guard at the switches in the railroad yards because of what we did there. Little things—all little things we did —but they have helped, I know."

"Now you can help us do big things," Dick said, "you and your friends in town. But there must be enemies, too—do you know them?"

"Oh, yes, I know them," the old man said grimly. "We have a list of them. Many have run away, to the north, afraid of the advancing Americans and afraid of their own townspeople, too. But there are a few left. There is Garone the banker and Balardi who was Mayor under Mussolini. He is still here. And they have a few sniveling underlings. But there are not many. Some there are who fear for their own necks. They will not actively fight the enemy, but they would never betray us, either."

"We'll put ourselves in your good hands," Dick said. "You can be our guide and helper here in Maletta."

"Is the town still the same?" Tony asked.

"No, of course not," Tomaso replied sadly. "Many have fled. Many others have been evacuated to the factories in the north. And all our young men— they were in the army, of course. Some are dead, others are prisoners of the Germans. We don't hear much. But here in Maletta we try to keep on laughing and smiling. Why, we still have the opera once a week."

He glanced apologetically at Dick. "I know that Ricardo Donnelli would find our opera company a poor one. Our costumes are shabby now, our sets falling to pieces. The good young voices are not here, but the performances still give us great joy—almost the only joy we still have in our lives."

"Then it is a fine opera company," Dick said. "If it gives the people pleasure, it is doing all that anything can do."

"Now tell me what I am to do," Tomaso said, in businesslike fashion.

"First, we must find a place for my radio," Tony said. "Uncle, I am a radioman for America's Army. We have, in the hills where we landed, a complete broadcasting set. I must use it to send messages in code to our Army, messages telling about movements of German troops and supplies through Maletta."

"That is not easy," Tomaso said, with a puzzled frown on his face. "The Germans do not like radios, even for receiving."

"They have a way, Uncle," Tony explained, "of listening to a radio and telling exactly where it is."

"I know, I know," the old man said. "The underground had a secret, illegal station in Florence—there are many others, but I know about this one. The Germans listened and found out exactly which block it was hidden in. Then they just went through all the houses and found it. There is another in a truck that moves from place to place, and they cannot find it. But the Germans have no detectors here in Maletta. I know that."

"They don't need to be right here," Tony said. "They might be in other towns, several miles away. They can pick up stations from a long distance. We cannot move about with our station. We cannot use it from the hills, for then the Germans would find our hiding place. Is there no place in the town itself where we can hide it? We need to use it only for a few minutes once or twice each day. But the hiding place must be absolutely safe—something the Germans just cannot locate."

The old man was thinking hard. He had offered to help. He could not fail to help in the very first thing they asked, no matter how difficult a task it was. But the town of Maletta—it had been gone over with a fine-tooth comb by the Germans many times. After each sabotage job, they went through every house, into wine cellars, into attics. After the Gestapo officer was killed they even tapped walls looking for hidden rooms.

He looked over the town as Dick and Tony waited for him to speak. The old man knew this town in which he had lived all his life, knew it as no one else did. There below him was the sprawling villa. Over to the right the railroad station. The three great church steeples loomed against the night sky just like the old bell tower over the villa.

Suddenly he gasped, and slapped his knee. Then he leaned back and laughed, almost soundlessly, but still with great good feeling. Dick and Tony looked at him in amazement. Dick wondered if something had cracked in the old man who had gone through so much. Maybe he was not completely dependable.

"Uncle Tomaso!" Tony was saying urgently. "What is it? What is it you're laughing about?"

"I'm laughing at what a good joke we shall play on the Germans!" the old man laughed. "I know where you can set up your radio!"

CHAPTER TEN

THE OLD BELL TOWER

"Right under our noses all this time," Tony's uncle said. "That's where we'll put your radio sending station, Tony my boy. And it will be right under—or rather, over—the Germans' noses, too!"

"Where?" the word came from both Tony and Dick at the same time.

"The old bell tower on the villa!" the old man declared, serious again.

"But that's been in ruins for years!" Tony objected.

"Exactly!" the old man agreed. "That's why it's so safe."

Dick was not sure he understood the old man.

"You mean that tall tower rising over the center of the villa?" he asked. "Is that the bell tower? I can just make it out."

"Yes, that's it!" Tomaso replied. "As Tony says, it has been in ruins for years—but it's still standing! That's the point—it is still standing there. Part of the stone top has crumbled away, where the bells used to be hundreds of years ago. That happened in another war long, long ago. The bells were taken from the tower and melted down. Later lightning struck the tower and knocked part of the top away. Finally, the stone stairway inside crumbled and fell. That was two hundred years ago, I'm told, and the caretaker of the villa in those days was killed by the falling stones inside the house."

"But the Nazis have taken over the villa!" Tony objected. "We can't put our radio up in the very headquarters of the Germans!"

"Why not?" Dick asked. He began to see why the old man laughed when he had this idea. "That's just about the last place they'd look—in their own headquarters."

"But the radio locating devices will place it there!" Tony pointed out.

"Of course," Dick agreed. "But if the Germans can't find the radio—then they'll know something's wrong. They'll search in all the buildings and houses near by and will find nothing. If the stone stairs into the tower have long been down, how can they get up there to look?"

"And if that's so, how can we get up there ourselves—with heavy radio equipment?" Tony demanded.

"Oh, we ought to be able to get up there some way," Dick said. "But the Germans won't think of it because—first, they just won't believe anyone would dare set up an illegal radio on top of their headquarters and, second, because to them there is no way to get there."

"That's right," Tomaso said. "When they first came to take over the villa, they looked everywhere. They wanted to be sure of the building they were moving into. They looked into every nook and cranny. They searched every room, looked up chimneys, investigated the big wine cellars, tried to find hidden passages and rooms. They asked a lot about the tower then. They know the stone stairs fell down two hundred years ago. They tried every possible way to get up—but they always tried from the *inside!* Finally they concluded no one could possibly get there. They never thought of the outside—and that's how you'll get there, Tony."

"But how?" the young radioman asked.

"I remember how agile you always were," Tomaso said. "I recall how you used to run down this hill and leap on the roof of the servants' wing. I know you could scale any wall, any tree!"

"That's right," Dick agreed. "Tony can get wherever he wants to go. He can crawl like a cat!"

"But not with a hundred or more pounds of radio under my arm," Tony objected. "You've a wonderful idea, I'll admit. Probably couldn't be a better place under the circumstances. Still, how can I get there and get the radio stuff there?"

"From the roof of the servants' wing," Tomaso said, "we can raise a ladder. The longest ladder we have is about fifteen feet long. That would still leave you fifteen feet from the opening at the top where the bells were."

"We can make an extension for the ladder," Dick said. "We can do that tomorrow in the woods, bring it down with us tomorrow night."

"Perhaps, perhaps," the old man said. "But it may not be very strong. Still, Tony is not heavy. If he also had a rope with a hook on the end, something that he could toss up to catch over the edge of the opening, then he could surely pull himself up."

"We could do that all right," Tony agreed. He was becoming more excited at the prospect of placing his radio over German headquarters.

"Then you could pull up the radio equipment with a rope," Dick said. "And one of us could climb up to help you. After all, you've got to have some one with you when you broadcast, to crank the generator handles and give you enough power."

"How do we know the tower is strong enough?" Tony asked.

"It is strong enough," the old man said. "It has stood all these years. A bolt of lightning did no more than knock a few rocks off the top."

"Won't we make a good deal of noise getting up there?" Dick asked.

"That is a chance we must take," Tomaso said. "But there are no Germans below the servants' wing. Then, too, the roof is very thick. I think they will not hear. We set our ladder up against the rear wall of the tower, so we cannot be seen from the front. We work after midnight when almost all are asleep, except the sleepy sentries and guards. They do not watch the villa closely—no, it is the railroad yards, the bridges, and the dam which they guard well."

Dick decided to go ahead with the old man's plan. They made arrangements to meet him the following night, shortly after midnight, behind the wing of the villa.

"There will be two more men with us then, Uncle Tomaso," Dick said. "So don't be startled when you see four figures on the hill here."

The man gave them his blessing, and the two Americans left, circling around the way they had come. It was close to midnight when they reached the cave in the hills where they found Vince Salamone and Max Burckhardt covering them with submachine guns as they approached. Slade was inside with Lieutenant Scotti.

"He's come to," Max said to Dick, "but he doesn't do much more than mumble yet. It first happened about half an hour ago."

Dick and Tony hurried inside, where they found Slade bending over the still prostrate figure of their lieutenant. Dick bent down beside him, and looked at Slade with questioning eyes.

"Don't know," the man shrugged. "He seems to see me, but there may be a little paralysis somewhere. He can't talk so that I can understand him, but his eyes seem clear. It's encouraging, anyway."

The light of a pocket flash gave Dick a chance to look into Scotti's face. The man's eyes opened slowly and he peered up. Dick flashed the light strongly on his own face so that Scotti could see him clearly.

"Jerry," he said. "Jerry, it's Dick."

Scotti's eyes looked straight and clear at his. Then his mouth opened a little and some sounds came out, but they meant nothing to Dick. Yet the look in the eyes showed Dick that the lieutenant recognized him, knew who he was. He felt sure that the wounded man could understand and hear everything, even if he could not speak.

"Jerry," he said, "you banged your head on a rock when you landed. You've been unconscious a long time. But everything is all right. The rest of us are together. We're in a good cave in the side of the hill. Everything is safe. Tony and I have been to Maletta. Tony's uncle is there, glad to help us. We'll set up the radio tomorrow night in town."

Dick saw the eyelids flicker up and down. It seemed to him that meant the lieutenant understood what had been said to him. Maybe he was just hoping that was the case, but somehow, Dick felt more as if the lieutenant were with them again.

"That's all for now," he said quietly. "You must rest more. For some reason you can't talk yet. Probably some pressure from the bang on the head. If you rest you'll be better tomorrow."

Once more the eyes flickered up and down as if the man were nodding his head. Dick turned out the light and went outside, followed by Boom-Boom Slade. There he told the others what he had said to the lieutenant.

"Somehow I think he got what I said," he explained. "Could that be possible, Slade?"

"From what I know, it could be," Slade replied. "And it may well be that he'll regain the ability to talk within a couple of days. I fed him a little something after he came to, and gave him some water, and he seemed to like that. From the look in his eyes he isn't suffering any great pain."

"In a week there'll be American Army doctors here," Tony said. "They can fix him up."

"You sound very certain about that," Max said. "You and Dick must have made out all right in town. How about it?"

Dick and Tony told the others about finding Uncle Tomaso and then about the plans for placing the radio in the old bell tower. At first they were incredulous, and then they all laughed just the way Uncle Tomaso had laughed.

"If that really works," Vince exclaimed, "it'll be the best joke the Germans ever had played on them. They think they're so smart! But it's just the sort of thing they'd never dream of doing—or of anybody else doing. By golly, I think we can really get away with it!"

"By Golly, I Think We Can Get Away With It!"

They talked for a long time. Slade wanted to know if they had looked at the dam, of course.

"No, not this trip," Dick replied. "But I did learn from Uncle Tomaso that it's pretty heavily guarded. There's a power station there, too. The underground has disrupted it a few times, so a sizable guard is around, I guess. It won't be easy to get a big load of dynamite planted in the right spot there. But—one problem at a time, I say. The radio is the first job, and we'll take care of that tomorrow night."

They finally went to sleep, and they slept late into the morning. Then they ate and sat around. Dick looked in at Lieutenant Scotti regularly, and he seemed better all the time. But his inability to speak seemed to bother him a great deal.

"Don't try to talk yet," Dick said. "It's too much for you."

This time, Scotti nodded his head slightly to show that he understood. So Dick proceeded to tell him about the plans for placing the radio in the bell tower. When he finished he asked, "Did you understand it all? Do you think it's okay?"

Again there was a slight nod of the head, and there seemed to be a smile in Scotti's eyes.

"I believe he thinks it's really a funny situation, too," Dick said to himself. "He'd like to laugh if he could, poor guy."

The day seemed endless for them all. They could do nothing but sit and wait for darkness. For men who loved action as these men did, it was difficult to sit still while there was so much to be done.

Even after darkness came, there was a long wait ahead of them, for they were not to meet Tomaso until after midnight. Every fifteen minutes from ten o'clock on, Vince or Max asked Dick if it weren't time to start yet. These two particularly were restless, for they had done nothing at all since their landing by parachute. Dick and Tony had at least gone into the town and laid plans.

It was well after eleven before Dick agreed to go. The radio equipment was packed and ready long before that. Vince had built a fifteen-foot ladder with an extra board at one end to enable it to fit over another ladder. They took rope and a sort of metal grappling hook which Max had hammered out of the metal cover of one of the supply containers.

Dick led the way down the hill, after telling Lieutenant Scotti that they were leaving, and getting a nod in reply. Slade wished them luck and sat by the entrance to the cave with a sub-machine gun across his knees.

The four men followed the same route Dick and Tony had taken the night before. Vince and Max would have gone at a trot, despite their heavy loads, if Dick had not held them back.

"I never saw two fellows so anxious to walk into an enemy-held town unarmed, and likely to be picked up and shot as spies!" the sergeant laughed.

"I just want to *do* something, that's all," Vince insisted.

"Sure, the general's depending on *us*, isn't he," Max added, "for the success of this whole operation?"

"Okay, okay," Dick said. "But the one way to make it a success is to take it easy except when fast action is called for. The main thing to remember tonight is—be quiet!"

They crossed the field and came to the road from the northeast. While Dick clambered up the ditch and looked up and down the highway, the rest of them crouched behind the wall with their loads. The lights of a car flickered a bit away from town, so Dick scurried back and joined the others behind the wall. In a few minutes four big trucks roared past them into the town. Dick jumped up, ran to the road again and motioned the others on.

Just as they were climbing over the wall on the other side, they heard again the sounds of motors and ducked down. This time half a dozen trucks came past and Dick whispered to Max, "Guess the general has started his attack. The reinforcements are beginning to come in."

In another fifteen minutes the four men stood on the hill behind the villa, near the clump of trees where Dick and Tony had talked with Tomaso the night before. Tony pointed out to Vince and Max the outline of the bell tower which rose high over the villa, and showed them the servants' wing at the rear of it, where they would put their ladders on the roof.

And then they saw the old man making his way up the hill toward them. They waited in silence until he came under the trees, and then Tony spoke.

"Hello, Uncle Tomaso," he said gently. "We're here."

"Yes, I see," the old man said. "With your radio—and a ladder, too."

"We have everything," Dick said. "And these are two more American soldiers. You may have heard of this big fellow—he's Vince Salamone."

The old man looked at the home-run king and his eyes shone!

"Of course!" he cried. "Who in the world does not know the world's greatest baseball player? You have won good-will for Italians everywhere, young man. Just think of it—here is old Tomaso with these two great men—Vincent Salamone and Ricardo Donnelli! I am most fortunate to be able to help you!"

"And this is Max Burckhardt," Dick said. "His family was German, so you can realize what a fighter he is against our enemies. But he cannot speak Italian. We will speak to him in English so he will understand."

The old man looked carefully at Max, who smiled

back at him, then nodded as if giving his approval.

"Come now," he said. "We will go to work."

"Is everything quiet?" Dick asked.

"Yes, but there has been much activity today," the old man said. "Many trucks and tanks and soldiers have come into Maletta by both roads. We have heard of a big attack by the American forces."

"Yes, that is why we must have the radio," Dick said. "We want to report to our Army how many trucks and tanks and soldiers come here. Can you learn that for us each day?"

"My friends and I—we can learn," Tomaso said. "Tomorrow morning I will tell them, and each evening I can give you the information. But I do not tell even my friends where the radio is. They need not know, and if the Germans should try to torture the information out of them, they will not be able to weaken."

They were led to the end of the wing where the old man pointed out a long ladder lying against the rear wall where there were no windows. Vince lifted it and placed it against the roof, which was only a few feet above them where they stood on the hill's side.

Dick went up first and stepped carefully on the roof. He was pleased to see that it was almost flat so that it would be easy not only to walk on, but also to set a ladder on. There was just a slight slope toward the rear.

He turned and motioned for the next man to follow, and Tony came up with one case of radio material. Then came the old man himself, and Dick and Tony helped him off the ladder. Next Max handed up the home-made ladder that Vince had put together that day, and Dick and Tony pulled it up and laid it on the roof. Max himself came next, with another box of radio material and the coil of rope with its metal grappling hook.

And last of all came Vince, with the big box containing the hand-cranked generator to supply power for the radio transmitter. When they were all on the roof, they waited for a minute, listening to see if there were any unusual sounds about. They heard the chugging of engines from the railroad yards to the west, the noise of truck motors coming down the road from the northwest, and that was all.

Dick and Tomaso walked along the roof side by side, treading lightly, and the others followed, bringing all equipment and both ladders. Finally they stood in the deep shadow at the base of the old bell tower. Looking up, it seemed to Dick as if it rose an impossible distance into the sky. He felt sure their ladders would never reach it.

Vince set to work fixing his home-made ladder to the end of Tomaso's ladder. It slid over the end all right, but was rather loose, so he took from his pocket a length of heavy cord and bound it round and round the shafts where both ladders were joined.

The others waited silently, watching him work quickly and surely. In two minutes the ladders were as strong as one long one, and Max helped Vince lift it so that they could lean it against the bell tower.

Dick stood back a little way to see how close it came to the opening near the top of the tower. It was almost ten feet short! He stepped forward and whispered to Vince and Max:

"Lean it at a sharper angle. It's short."

He stepped back and saw that the new position gained only about three feet. The top rung was still about seven feet below the opening in the tower. And Tony could never stand on the top rung, hugging the wall. He'd have to stand on the third rung from the top, so he'd have some support for his hands and could lean his body in against the wall. Of course, there was the rope and grappling hook, but that was tricky business—uncertain and likely to make a good deal of noise.

Vince was standing beside him. "Can't make it any steeper," he said. "It would topple backward."

"Then Tony will have to try that rope and grappling hook," Dick said. They stepped forward to the others again.

"Tony, you'll have to try that rope trick," Dick said. "But make it as quiet as possible, please. We'll steady the ladder for you down here, and we'll even try to catch you if you fall. But take it easy. It will probably take you quite a few tries before you can hook that thing on the edge. We don't know if it's big enough to grab hold of that rock at the opening. Maybe you can't make it at all."

"I'll do my best," Tony said, taking the rope and the hook from Max, who had tied the metal piece to the end of the rope. Tony slung the coil over his shoulder and started up the ladder. Without a sound he slicked up the wobbly steps as if he were sliding, not climbing.

"Look at 'im go," Max whispered. "He's a wonder, that guy."

Dick just looked upward without a word. Then he felt the old man's hand clutch his arm. Still he did not take his eyes away from Tony.

"Don't worry, Tomaso," he said. "Tony will be all right."

"Yes, Tony is a good boy," the old man said, and took his hand away.

Tony was near the top now. Dick could see the black blob that was his figure against the wall of the tower. He saw an arm swing outward and heard the clink of metal against stone. It was not as loud a noise as he had thought it would be, and he breathed a little more easily. He watched the arm swing outward again. There was another metallic sound, and this time Dick saw the spark as metal hit stone. It seemed to him, as clearly as he could make out, that Tony had come close that time. But he was hoping so hard that he felt he must be wishing it to catch hold.

Again Tony swung the rope with the big hook on the end. Each time he felt the ladder wobble, each time he grabbed with one hand to steady himself, each time he was sure he was falling. And then, each time, too, he had to dodge that big metal hook that hurtled down at him when it missed catching. He had not only to dodge it, but to try to catch it so it would not clatter against the wall and make too much noise.

After half a dozen tries he stopped. His heart was beating like a trip-hammer, and his breath was coming short. He knew that the others below were tense.

He pulled himself together and tried again. The hook missed and came down again. He caught it, almost lost his balance, grabbed hold, and threw again. He was already ducking and reaching out for the falling hook before he realized that this time it was not falling. It had caught over the edge!

"Boy, I hate to give a tug on this rope," he said to himself. "I'm afraid if I do it will come right down again."

But he tugged a little bit. The hook did *not* come down. He tugged harder. Still it did not come down. Then with both hands he pulled. It was secure.

As a final test, he lifted his feet from the ladder rung and let the rope support his whole body. He wanted to shout with joy at knowing that he had succeeded, but he could only smile silently.

Below, Dick knew that Tony had made it. There was no more slinging of that big hook. Then he watched Tony's figure creep up the side of the wall above the ladder. Maybe the hook had been caught —but what if it gave way now? Tony would topple down in their midst, the ladders would fall, the metal hook would clatter to the roof, and the sentries would be shooting at them!

But it didn't happen. Instead he saw Tony's figure disappear—and that could mean only one thing! He had crawled in through the opening in the bell tower. He had made it!

CHAPTER ELEVEN

FRUITLESS SEARCH

The men on the roof said no word. They all knew, even old Tomaso, that Tony had reached the opening at the top of the bell tower. They stood close to the wall, their eyes fixed upward. For almost five minutes they did not hear a sound or see anything.

Dick knew that Tony was busy. First, he was feeling his way about in the darkness up there. At some point in the tower there was the yawning hole of the ancient stone staircase which had crumbled so long ago. Tony had to locate that danger spot and make sure to keep away from it. Then he had to find a strong beam or rock to which he might tie the end of the rope for pulling up his supplies. Dick wondered if any part of the old bell stanchions might still be standing.

Suddenly a figure leaned from the opening at the top of the tower, and then the rope came sliding down the wall toward them. At a whispered word Vince and Max removed the long ladder from the side of the tower and placed it flat on the roof, out of the way. Dick, meanwhile, grabbed the rope end and tied it securely to the first container holding radio material. Then he gave three short tugs on the rope.

It started upward at once. Tony took it slowly so that the container would not bump noisily against the wall. Even with the greatest care, it made too much noise as it scraped upward. Dick was worried about it. He turned to Vince and Max.

"This might bring somebody out to see what's going on," he whispered. "You'd better get going. No use all of us taking a chance on getting caught. Take the ladders back. Take them apart. Vince, you take your ladder and the cord you used back to the cave. Help Tomaso put his ladder back where it belongs—not near this wing, anyway. The Germans will be looking around for a radio transmitter tomorrow and we want to leave no clues for them."

"Okay, Dick," Vince said, picking up the long ladder.

"See that Tomaso gets back to his room," Dick said. "Then you and Max head for the cave. When I get all the supplies up there, I'm going up with Tony. As soon as he gets the radio working we'll get in touch with our forces, send our first message. I'll stick there with Tony until after dark tomorrow evening. Then I'll get back to the cave. See you there. If Scotti's all right, give him a report on what we've done."

While Dick was giving these instructions, the first container had scraped up the tower wall to the opening and Tony had pulled it inside. Now the rope was let down to the roof once more, and Dick quickly tied the end to the second container as Max and Vince went to the rear of the roof with Tomaso. Dick gave three jerks on the rope and the second container started upward.

He looked back and saw the last of the three figures disappear from the roof at the rear of the wing. He listened carefully but could hear no sound other than the scraping of the metal container as it scratched its way up to Tony. Then, when Tony pulled it inside, there was complete silence. There was no indication that any of the Germans had heard the sound and were coming to investigate.

In a few minutes the rope came snaking down the tower wall for the last, and heaviest, container. It took Dick some time to tie it securely, for it was an odd shape. He wondered if Tony would have too hard a time pulling it up. Tony was small, but he was wiry and strong.

Just before he pulled his signal on the rope, he heard a slight sound somewhere behind him. He jerked around, startled, and then saw two shadows making their way across the hill behind the villa.

"Just Max and Vince," Dick sighed with relief to himself. "If anything happens now, they're in the clear at least and can carry on."

He pulled the rope and the big container started upward. A foot at a time it went, scraping more noisily than either of the other boxes. Halfway up

Dick Tied the Rope Securely Around the Box

it stopped for a full minute.

"Tony's tired," Dick told himself. "He's probably taking an extra turn around his post with the rope, in case his arms give out at the crucial moment."

Then the box started upward again at a pace which seemed painfully slow to Dick, standing alone on the roof below. Almost inch by inch it scratched toward the opening. Then it was there! Tony was pulling it inside, Dick saw, but then there was a sudden loud clanking noise.

Instinctively, Dick crouched against the wall. The big box must have slipped a bit as Tony tried to haul it inside. But he caught it, dragged it in. That noise—it had been loud. Surely it would bring someone to look around!

The rope slid down the wall quickly, and Dick snatched at it the moment it was within reach. Hand over hand he pulled himself up the wall, bracing his feet against the stone and walking up. Halfway up he was panting, and the rope began to cut into his hands. But he did not let himself slow down. If only he could get up there fast enough—

He felt a hand grasp his arm and knew that Tony was leaning out to help him inside. With another pull he was able to throw one hand over the stone ledge. Then, with a terrific heave, he slid his body through the opening, tumbling onto the stone floor inside and banging his head against a huge wooden beam.

FRUITLESS SEARCH 173

Tony was already pulling the rope in as fast as he could, and Dick sat where he had fallen, trying to get his breath back, not daring to move yet for fear he might fall into the stair well. Then Tony was on the floor beside him, whispering.

"Good going, Dick!" he said. "Sorry I made such a clatter. I almost went out the opening with that last container. Keep to this side. The stair well is there on your right, up against that wall. Everything else is safe. There are big beams in the center where the bells used to be. That's where I tied the rope."

"And where I banged my head," Dick added. "Wait—what's that?"

They froze in their tracks and listened. Below they heard voices, one commanding, the other replying—in German. Tony moved silently to an opening at the front of the tower, and Dick followed him. Looking down, they could see a lighted space in front of the villa, with light coming from two windows and the open door.

A German officer stood there, giving orders to two sentries. They were walking to the sides of the villa, throwing their strong flashlight beams into every dark corner and shadow.

"They heard it," Dick whispered. "They're looking around to see what's what."

"What about the others?" Tony asked.

"Safely away," Dick said. "And Tomaso's in his

room."

They watched as the sentries circled around to the wing at the rear of the villa, then returned and made a report to the officer. They threw their flashlight beams upward toward the roof, over the old bell tower and across the street. But there was nothing to be found. In a moment the officer went back inside and the sentries took up their regular posts at the front of the villa. The lights went out, and Dick and Tony turned to each other and smiled.

"Now to work," Tony said. "I'll get that radio set up."

Tony worked in the dark. It was not for nothing that he had so carefully practiced assembling this radio. He wanted to be able to do it by feeling alone, without relying on any light. Dick helped by holding the few tools in his hands and giving them to Tony when he asked for them. When Tony finished with the screwdriver he returned it to Dick's hands, so no time would be wasted feeling around for it.

It took almost an hour for Tony to complete his work. During that time he worked without pause, muttering to himself the names of the different parts he handled, giving himself instructions. Dick sat patiently and said nothing, knowing Tony's complete concentration on his job. Finally, the young radioman turned to Dick and said, "There! It's done. If it will only work now."

"Want the light for a few minutes to check it?"

FRUITLESS SEARCH

Dick asked. "I think it might be safe."

"No, I'm pretty sure it's okay," Tony replied. "After that noise, those sentries may be more on the alert than usual."

Dick edged his way up to the generator and felt for the cranks. "Tell me when to start turning," he said.

"Okay," Tony said. "Give me some power now."

Dick turned the cranks and got them going at a regular speed.

"That's about right," Tony said. Dick heard him snap a switch and speak in a clear voice into the little microphone.

"Julius Caesar to Mark Antony," he said. "Julius Caesar to Mark Antony."

Over and over he repeated the words, and after the tenth repetition, he got his answer through his earphones.

"Mark Antony to Julius Caesar," the voice said. "Come in, Julius Caesar."

"Got it, Dick," Tony whispered exultantly. "Now give me the message—in Italian and in code. I'll repeat."

Dick had memorized most of the short code which had been devised in Italian for these special reports, so that he would not have to use a light to refer to a code book. Later, he knew, when he came to give detailed information as to troops and equipment, he would have to refer to his code book to get things absolutely straight. But now he just wanted headquarters to know that the paratroop party was established in Maletta.

He spoke softly to Tony the words which would tell the American general that the party had landed safely except for Scotti's accident, that they had contacted Tony's uncle, that the radio was now set up in the town itself. The next report, to come at eight o'clock the next evening, would give detailed information about German troop movements into Maletta, some of which had already started.

And that was all. It was essential to keep on the air the shortest possible time, so that the German locator stations would have only a minute or two in which to get a fix on the illegal transmitter.

Dick and Tony sat back. There was nothing more for them to do for a long time, and they knew it.

"But I'll bet there's a lot going on in certain places," Dick said to Tony. "Back at headquarters, for instance, the radio orderly has rushed that message to the code room and it will be taken at once to the general. I'll bet he left word to be awakened at any time a message came through from us."

"And they're plenty busy at a couple of German listening posts, too," Tony said. "Maybe we'll see some of the fun."

Tony was right. In four German monitor stations their message had been heard. In each one a line had been drawn on a detailed map showing the direction from which the radio report had come. The message itself, in Italian, was obviously code, and was rushed to decoding experts.

There were telephone calls from the four monitor stations to Gestapo headquarters in a city to the northwest of Maletta. There the four lines of the four different stations were drawn on a map, and the spot at which those lines crossed was in the town of Maletta.

Before dawn two big black cars roared out of the city, toward Maletta itself. That town, now the crucial point of resistance to the American Army's northward drive, would not have an illegal radio station for long, the Gestapo officers felt sure. It was important—so important that Colonel Klage himself led the locating party to wipe out that new station which was obviously trying to get vital information to the Americans.

At that time, Dick and Tony were asleep in the bell tower, after having eaten a light meal from their ration tins. But the first light of dawn woke them. Even if it had not, the roar of the two speeding cars stopping in front of the villa would have done so. They peered cautiously down out of the opening at the front of the tower.

Germans poured from the two big black cars, and one banged noisily on the door of the villa after showing his credentials to the sentries there. A man in a colonel's uniform was looking over the villa and then at the houses across the street. Dick could not see his face, but he knew that the man was looking quite bewildered. He was standing at the exact spot shown on the map to be the location of the illegal transmitter—and yet it was German Army headquarters!

Two or three officers poured out of the front door of the villa, some of them still pulling on jackets. Dick and Tony saw that some were in their slippers, and they did not look at all smart. Instead they were perturbed, even though officers of rank a good deal higher than the colonel who faced them. A colonel in the Gestapo could still make an army general tremble.

Dick wished that he might have heard the conversation that was going on below: the angry statement of the colonel that an illegal transmitter had operated from that spot and the vigorous protestations of the others that such a thing was impossible. The colonel took a map from an aide and pointed out the exact spot of the radio station, proving that it was in German army headquarters in Maletta.

The army men pointed to houses across the street, and down the road to the right. They were saying, Dick knew, that the transmitter must be there, somewhere else in the neighborhood.

Then the search began. The Gestapo men went first to the small house directly across the street from the villa. They were there half an hour, and

FRUITLESS SEARCH

Dick and Tony knew how thoroughly they were tearing that home to pieces looking for the hidden radio.

"I hate to put these Italians through such an ordeal," Dick whispered, "but we can't help it."

"In a while they will know the reason for it all," Tony said, "and then they will not mind what they are going through now."

Dick and Tony felt that they had box seats at a good show that day. All morning and well into the afternoon the search went on. Houses and stores and buildings within several blocks were searched thoroughly, and finally the villa itself was gone over inch by inch, despite the protestations of the German army men that the Gestapo officer was insulting them by searching in their own headquarters for an illegal Italian radio. But the Gestapo colonel did not care how many people he insulted. He knew what would happen to him if he returned to his own headquarters without having found and destroyed that transmitter. And he knew how silly it would sound to his superior officer when he said that his locators had placed the radio in German army headquarters in Maletta.

He himself began to doubt the accuracy of his listening posts. But for four of them to go wrong at the same time—that was impossible! There was something radically wrong somewhere and the colonel didn't like it one bit. His anger was apparent even to Tony and Dick as they watched him get into his big black car, slam the door, and pull away with tires screaming as the cars careened around the corner.

"The colonel is a bit miffed," Tony said, with a happy smile.

"He'll be more than miffed in a few days," Dick said. "Before the week is out that guy's going to be in a real predicament."

CHAPTER TWELVE

A VISIT TO THE DAM

Although Dick and Tony had been entertained by the vain search of the Germans for their radio, they did not fail to note the increasing movement of troops and equipment into Maletta. Trucks came down both main roads into the town, and the Americans could see them both for some distance from their vantage point high in the bell tower. The road to the northeast, leading past the dam, they had already seen when they crossed it at night coming down from their cave in the hills. Now they could see where it climbed up to circle around the dam itself.

In the other direction they saw the northwest road, over which most of the supplies were now coming. It passed through a narrow gorge just outside of the little town, a pass made by the ridge of hills on the western edge of Maletta valley, and the single big hill at the head of the town, against which the villa was built. The northwest road had to climb this fairly steep hill to get through the pass.

"When we get a chance," Dick said to Tony, "I'd like to have a look at that road up there. It looks as if it might go through a narrow pass that could easily be blown up. I'm not forgetting that Slade has a good deal of extra dynamite, and I'd like to put it to good use."

"The dam comes first, though, doesn't it?" Tony asked.

"Yes, of course, the dam is the most important," Dick said, "but if we could cut off the German line of escape up the northwest road, it would be mighty good!"

Dick and Tony saw that most of the truckloads of soldiers that came into town went right on through, heading down the valley to the south to reinforce the men there beating off the American frontal attack. Tanks, both light and heavy, rumbled along the roads, too, and huge 155-millimeter howitzers were towed slowly by tractors.

They got a complete report on the German troop movements shortly after dark that evening, when old Tomaso crept forward to the bell tower on the roof of the rear wing of the villa. Dick let down the rope quickly, waited a moment, and then felt three jerks. He pulled it up again and found a sheet of paper tied to the end. He was unfolding the sheet of paper when he saw the dark figure of the old Italian creep back along the roof and disappear at the end.

"This is just what we want," Dick said to Tony. "Your uncle has some good friends that really know

Dick Read the Report of German Troop Movements

their stuff."

"Well, he probably has the local policeman and the grocer and a few others looking and listening," Tony said. "And I imagine Tomaso himself overhears a good deal when he's cleaning up in Army headquarters below us."

Dick got down on the floor of the tower and got out his flashlight. Tony stood over him so as to prevent as much as possible of the light from showing. Even then, Dick covered the front of the flash with his shirt so that only a faint glow came through on to the paper. But it was enough to read by, and enough to show him what code words he should use in making his radio report.

"The fourteenth motorized division has come through today," Dick said to Tony. "In addition there's a panzer force of forty small and twenty large tanks. Eighteen pieces of heavy artillery have gone through and are being emplaced about three miles south of the town."

"The floods will get every one of those," Tony cried. "The Germans certainly do think we're making our big push right straight up the valley. They're pouring everything in here to stop it."

"Okay now, Tony," Dick said. "I've got all the code words in my mind. Let's give our report and, incidentally, set the Gestapo on their ears again."

They went to the radio and Dick began to crank the generator. In a moment, Tony had made contact with the American Army headquarters and repeated clearly the code words that Dick spoke to him. Then he repeated all again and shut off the radio.

"I'll be leaving you now, Tony," Dick said, standing up. "I've got lots of work to do tonight."

"Wish I could help you," Tony said.

"Same here, but somebody's got to stay here with the radio," Dick replied. "We've got to have someone to keep his eyes on the town, somebody who can get a message from Tomaso in case anything important turns up, and especially someone to let down the rope when necessary. If we both left, we'd have to leave the rope hanging here for us to get back up again, and that's out of the question."

"Sure, I understand," Tony said, as Dick climbed to the ledge and tossed out the rope to the roof below. "I'll stick by my radio. What about the next report?"

"Either Vince or I will come shortly before dawn," Dick said, "when Tomaso sends up his next report. The schedule is each evening after dark, each morning before dawn—unless something comes up to prevent it."

"In a pinch I can turn the generator and handle the radio at the same time," Tony said. "It's not easy but I *can* do it if I have to."

"Maybe you *will* have to some time," Dick said. "But there'll be somebody here with you as much as possible. So long, Tony."

"Good luck, Dick," the radioman replied, and Dick slipped down the rope to the roof. Then Tony pulled the rope up again and settled down for the night as he saw Dick's shadowy figure making off across the hill at the rear.

Dick's first inquiry as he approached the cave in the hills was about Lieutenant Scotti.

"He's talking some," Slade reported. "It's not easy, but he can move around a bit. I really think he's coming along okay. There may have been some internal bleeding that caused some pressure against the brain, but that's stopping now. Anyway, he's anxious to see you. He knows about getting the radio up in the bell tower and he's delighted."

With a nod to Vince and Max, Dick went on in the cave and knelt down beside Scotti. The wounded man smiled a little and his eyes shone.

"Dick," he said, and that was all. Dick saw that it was a great effort for him to speak.

"Wonderful to see you getting better, Jerry," he said, "but don't try to talk too much. Let me do most of the talking and you answer with nods as much as you can."

Dick then told his lieutenant about the safe installation of the transmitter in the bell tower, about getting the first message through to American headquarters, then about the frantic search by the Germans for the illegal radio. At this, Scotti started to laugh but it hurt his head too much and he stopped. But Dick saw that he thought it was a wonderful joke on the so-smart Germans.

Dick went on to tell Jerry about the movement of German troops and supplies through the town, the detailed reports given them by Tomaso, and the second radio report that had been sent in just a short while before.

"You're doing wonderful job," Scotti said slowly and with great effort. "Keep it up!"

"Sure," Dick said. "We'll carry on, and I feel better now because I can tell you our plans, and you can tell me if you think I'm doing right or not. Now we've got to have a look at the dam. I'm taking Slade and Vince with me to look it over so Slade can decide where his dynamite charge must be placed, and I can figure out how to handle the guard so he can get in to do it. It won't be easy. Max will stay here with you until we get back. Tony's in the bell tower with the radio."

Scotti nodded his approval of these plans and Dick gave him a pat on the shoulder and moved away. At the front of the cave he found the others and gave them the latest news.

"Now we're going to look at the dam," he said, and Slade sighed with relief.

"I was beginning to wonder," he said, "when we would get around to the main objective of this mission."

Dick laughed. "Okay, Boom-Boom, tonight is your night. Vince will come along with us. Max, you stay here with Scotti until we get back."

The three men started down the hill from the cave. But this time they did not go as far as the field below. Instead, they kept to the woods and circled around to the east where the hill ended at the right-hand branch of the Y which was the northeastern branch of the Maletta valley. It took them almost an hour to reach the dam, for they were not always sure of their direction.

It was the glinting of a light on the water of the artificial lake that finally told them it was near at hand. They moved forward much closer to the edge of the trees and looked down. From where they stood, on the hill a little above the dam, they had a perfect view of everything.

Directly below them about seventy-five feet was the main northwest road which went part way up the hill in order to circle around the dam and lake. On the other side of the road there was a short drive which led in toward the dam itself, which was a concrete structure about three hundred yards long, stretching to the opposite hill. On top of the dam wall at this end was a concrete building and near it stood several sentries.

"Probably the control house for the sluice gates," Slade said, "and headquarters for the guards. There's a similar structure at the other end of the wall, but smaller."

Below the dam itself, on a stretch of level ground, stood the electric power station. It was a low building made of brick, about fifty feet square.

"Not a big plant at all," Slade told Dick, "but I imagine in the present battle emergency it's pretty important as a source of electric power for the Germans."

Dick and Vince nodded, watching Slade as he looked over the objective with a practised eye. There was a long black steel pipe, at least ten feet in diameter, leading from the bottom of the dam to the power house. That, Dick knew, was the sluice, or pipe-line, which carried the water under pressure into the power house for turning the turbines that drove the generators.

"It won't be easy," Slade said. "Even figuring that you can get me in there despite all those guards, it's going to be tough to place the charge so that it will surely knock the dam completely out and not just crack it."

"Tell me the place you want to put your dynamite," Dick said, "and then it's up to me to get you there."

He knew that was a broad statement, for he still had no idea how he could get Slade and his dynamite past the guards on the wall and around the power house.

"There *is* one spot that would do the job, without

a doubt," Slade said. "But I'm afraid that would be asking too much of you. Do you see that pipe-line over there?"

"Yes, I see it," Dick replied.

"Well, if I could get inside that and crawl up to where it comes out of the dam itself, it would work," Slade said. "With the big pipe coming out of it, that's the weakest part of the whole structure. But that pipe is filled with water under very high pressure."

"Wow! That's a tough assignment all right," Dick said. "But let's see—what if the pipe didn't have any water in it?"

"You mean if the water-gate at the entrance to the pipe were closed?" Slade asked. "If that were done, I could get there all right. All those pipes have a couple of hatch-like openings along them so that workmen can get in to clean them out and so on."

"Then you wouldn't have to go through the power house itself?" Dick asked.

"No, I could get in the pipe, I'm sure, not far from the spot where it enters the dam," Slade answered. "And I could place the dynamite right under the weak spot of the dam. But the water-gate would have to stay shut completely until after the charge was exploded."

"I see," Dick said. "Let me think that one over a bit. You go on getting the lay of the land completely

A VISIT TO THE DAM

in your mind."

Slade and Vince continued their observations while Dick tried to figure out a way to get Slade and his dynamite into the pipeline. Suddenly he remembered something that Tomaso had said to him on the first night they talked together.

"Boom-Boom," Dick called to Slade, "tell me something. If for some reason the turbines or dynamos were damaged badly and the plant had to shut down for a few days, would they close the water-gate leading from the dam through the pipe-line?"

"Of course they would," Slade replied. "That's the first thing they'd do. And they wouldn't open it again until all repairs were made."

"There's our answer," Dick exclaimed. "Old Tomaso told me that the underground has several times performed a little neat sabotage at this power station, stopping it for several days until repairs were made. If they did it before, they ought to be able to do it again."

"Swell," Slade said. "Then I could really do the job—*provided* we can get through all those guards, place the ammunition, lead out my wires and hook them up to a detonator."

"All right, I'll have to figure that out, too," Dick said. "But I can't see how yet. We'll just have to find some way, but for the life of me I don't see what it can be. Anyway, we've solved part of our problem. We'll get our dam blown up right and proper, boys, and don't you ever forget it. But we can't waste very much time. Tonight is already the third night. We have just three nights more in which to do our work!"

CHAPTER THIRTEEN

THE FOURTH NIGHT

Halfway back to the cave, Dick suddenly felt exhausted. He realized that he had had very little sleep and not a great deal to eat.

"Vince," he said, "will you go down to the bell tower and stay with Tony? He'll be on the lookout for someone before long and will let the rope down to you. Tomaso will come with the latest reports just before dawn, and you can crank the generator for Tony while he gives his radio report to our headquarters. Tony has the code book. Tell him to add, in addition to Tomaso's details on troop movements, that we've figured how to blow up the dam."

"Okay, Sarge," Vince said. "But that's putting yourself out on a limb. Then you'll really *have* to figure out how to do it!"

"That's the point," Dick said. "If I've committed myself to the general, then I'll make myself come through somehow. Okay, Vince, on your way. Duck out before it gets light and come back to the cave."

Vince walked down the hill toward the road and the town, as Slade and Dick circled around the hill toward their cave.

"How much dynamite will you have left over

after placing the charge in the dam?" Dick asked.

"About half of it," Slade replied.

"Good. Then tomorrow you can teach me the ropes on how to place a charge, attach fuses, wires and detonators. You've got two sets of everything, haven't you?"

"Sure I have," the demolition man replied. "What else are you planning on blowing up?"

"Not sure yet," Dick said. "I'll tell you after I take a little trip tonight. Right now I'm too tired to do anything."

When they returned to the cave, Dick found that Scotti was sleeping soundly, so he did not report to him then about their observations at the dam. Instead, he stretched out and fell into a deep sleep almost at once. Despite all the difficulties confronting him, he could sleep. He knew he had to if he were to be fit and able to solve all his problems.

The sun was high in the sky when he awoke. He had not heard Vince return from town, nor the others eating their breakfast. But he felt completely refreshed and ready to tackle anything. After washing his face and hands, he went in to Scotti and told him all the news, including that brought by Vince about the latest radio report to headquarters, which had gone smoothly. Scotti was better, finding it possible to talk more easily and without the great effort of the day before. He was now propped up against the wall of the cave, with nylon parachutes behind him.

"You'd better get out in the sun a bit," Dick suggested.

"It would be good," Scotti replied. So Dick called Vince and Max, and the two big men carried their lieutenant gently outside and placed him near the entrance to the cave. Then he joined Dick in a bite to eat and listened to their plans.

Dick told about the dam, and explained that he had to find some way to draw the guards away before Slade could get in with his dynamite.

"I'm sure Tomaso can get the sabotage work done all right," he said, "so that the water will be shut off. But then the guard might even be increased at the dam. If we could go in and do it at the last minute, we might be able just to mow the guards down with our guns. But we can't take that chance. We've got to be *sure!* That means we ought to get in there and get our dynamite placed the night before the explosion."

Scotti thought the problem over but could not come up with an answer. Slade did not even try to figure it out. He was too busy going over in his mind how he would crawl up that pipe and place his dynamite charges. It was Max who finally made a very timid suggestion.

"Dick," he said, "this may sound like a fairy-tale idea, but maybe it would work. Remember we were kidding about wearing Italian peasants' clothes when we first got here and we said something about swiping a German uniform for me? Well, if your Uncle Tomaso could get a really good officer's uniform, I might be able to march right up and give those guards a few orders and so get them out of the way for a while."

"That would be dangerous as the devil!" Dick replied.

"Of course it would," Max said. "But this whole operation is dangerous. If it doesn't work it means I get caught, that's all. But if it does work, we'll get our dynamite in place. We can figure out exactly what to do, all right."

"Maybe so," Dick said. "At least it's an idea. What do you think of it, Scotti?"

The lieutenant shrugged his shoulders as if to say he did not know. Then he spoke.

"Depends on rank of officer in charge of guards at dam," he said haltingly. "Also on rank of uniform Max would wear. He must be able to awe everyone at dam completely so they do not question his word at all."

"Well, we can find out about that after the dam is sabotaged," Dick said. "Tomaso will be able to tell us the details about the guard there the next day. And he'll be the one to get us the uniform. We can tell him to try to get a good one."

"Suggest you ask him to do that," Scotti said. "Then Max will have uniform if we can think of

"If I Could Only Get a German's Uniform!"

no other solution."

"Right, Scotti," Dick answered. "I'll do that when I see Tomaso tonight. Meanwhile, we'll all be thinking of some other plan that might work."

Dick noticed that Scotti was looking tired and in some pain.

"You'd better get back inside now," he said, "and lie down for a real rest. You've got to take it easy. But I feel a lot better being able to go over these things with you."

After Jerry was settled comfortably in the cave again, Dick went outside with Boom-Boom Slade, who proceeded to give him a lesson in demolition, explaining just how to place the charge and attach the detonator. Dick spent the afternoon going over the lessons he had learned.

After dark, Dick, Max, and Slade set out for the town, while Vince stayed behind with Lieutenant Scotti. As they approached the villa, they saw that there were many cars parked in front and there seemed to be many lights inside the front rooms. In the servants' wing, however, there was nothing but a faint glow from old Tomaso's room.

"Seems to be plenty going on there," Max said. "Think it's safe to go up to Tony so early?"

"Sure," Dick said. "They're too noisy and too busy to look on their own rear roof. But you and Slade stay back here in the trees and wait for me. Tomaso will be coming back after a while, too, and

I must talk to him."

Dick went forward alone, got on the low roof and went forward quickly to the bell tower. Tony had apparently been on the lookout, for the rope was waiting for Dick when he got there. In another two minutes he was inside the tower with Tony.

"They've been tearing this town to pieces today," Tony said. "Looking for our transmitter, of course. They've even sent some details down into the sewers around here. They haven't even bothered around the villa itself, though, except once when that Gestapo colonel asked about this bell tower. They took him inside and showed him the ruined steps. I could hear their voices up here as they looked up, with a flashlight shooting around. Of course they couldn't see anything, and the colonel was convinced."

"How long do you think he'll stay convinced?" Dick asked.

"I don't know," Tony replied. "It looks as if he's moved right in here permanently. I've kept my eyes open, and they haven't come in with a radio locator on a truck. When they do that, we'll have to watch our step, maybe cut down our reports to once a day and vary the times a little bit."

"We'll see," Dick replied. "Now I want to write a note to Tomaso before he comes, telling him to meet us in the trees behind the villa in a little while."

He scribbled the note on a piece of paper and tied it to the end of the rope just in time, as he saw the figure of the old man creeping forward along the roof. Looking down as he tossed the rope down, Dick saw Tomaso take the note from the rope, then attach his own paper to it and give three jerks.

After studying Tomaso's details on the day's movements of German troops and equipment, Dick and Tony made their report to American headquarters. And at the last moment, Dick decided to tell them the broadcast schedule would be changed for safety's sake. The next report would be at one A.M. the following night.

"That's a good idea," Tony said, after they had switched off the radio. "They're bound to get mobile locators here tomorrow anyway. And they'll be listening especially after dusk and just before dawn, when we've broadcast before. If we go on the air at one in the morning for only about two minutes, they won't have time to do much of anything."

"Sorry you've got to stay here all the time, Tony," Dick said, as he prepared to leave. "But it's the only thing to do."

He gave the radioman the latest news of the dam, of Scotti, and their plans.

"They're actually giving an opera here in town tomorrow night," Tony said. "Wish I could hear it. I think it's wonderful the way they won't let anything stop their opera!"

"Opera seems a million miles away from me right now," Dick said. "It's hard to remember that I ever sang in opera. Well—maybe I'll sneak in for a look tomorrow night if I haven't anything else to do."

He laughed, and then crawled over the ledge and let himself down the rope to the roof below. Crouching low, he made his way back to the end of the wing, dropped off, and scurried up the hill to the clump of trees. There he found old Tomaso waiting with Max and Slade.

"Tomaso," Dick said, "you are doing a wonderful job. Your reports are perfect—just what we want. They are of very great help to our Army."

The old man beamed with pleasure. "It is my friends, too. They know the information is for the Americans, who will soon be here to free us."

"Now I must ask two more big things of you and your friends," Dick said. "And for these I must tell you of our plans. Two nights from now, just before dawn, we plan to blow up the dam!"

"The dam!" Tomaso exclaimed. "Why — the town will be washed away!"

"Yes, Tomaso," Dick said. "But with the town will go thousands of German soldiers, hundreds of trucks, tanks, guns, and many supplies. The German Army will be trapped and defeated. When the flood waters recede you will have your town again, and there will be no more Germans here. Won't it be worth it?"

The old man thought a moment. "Yes," he finally said. "It will be worth it. Of course. If the town were to be wiped off the map forever, it would be all right if it meant we got rid of the Germans. But what about the people here?"

"Your own people must be warned in time so they can get to the hills," Dick replied. "But not too long in advance must they know, lest some word leak out. Tonight you can tell those closest to you, those who can surely be trusted completely. Then, on the night before the wrecking of the dam, these can pass the word to all others. They must filter out into the hills, trying their best to cause no wonderment among the Germans."

"I understand," the old man said. "We shall do as you wish. But you said there were two other things to do."

"Yes, to help us blow up the dam," Dick said. He explained that Slade must be able to get into the pipe-line from the dam and for that the power plant must be damaged so the water-gates would be shut off for a few days.

"You said that your people had damaged the power plant before," Dick went on. "Can they do it again, tomorrow?"

The old man thought for a few minutes. "Yes," he said, "I believe they can. You see, there are now only a few Italians allowed to work there. Those are on the day shift. Only Germans are there at night.

But one of our men there has been experimenting. He told me that he had discovered that a wrench set on a certain ledge near the big dynamo would gradually move, from the vibration, and fall into the mechanism in about fifteen minutes. His idea was to place some tools on that spot just before he left work. Then, if none of the night men saw them within fifteen minutes, they would topple into the dynamo. And they would surely damage it badly. You see, they could not blame it on the Italians, because no Italians would be around at the time it happened. He wanted to find some way to wreck the machinery without having a few hostages shot as a result. That's what happened the last time."

"It sounds perfect," Dick said. "Will he try it tomorrow?"

"When he knows who asks it," Tomaso replied, "he will do it. He is now the tenor in our little opera company and he will do anything for Ricardo Donnelli. And after doing that he will sing even better in the performance tomorrow night."

Dick smiled.

"What are they performing tomorrow night?" he asked.

"*Pagliacci*," Tomaso replied. "Nowadays we can give only short performances."

"Now for the second request," Dick said. "We must find some way to get our men to the pipe-line at the dam, which is well guarded. It may be guarded even more completely after the sabotage tomorrow. So—you know that this man, Max Burckhardt, speaks German. If he could appear at the dam in the uniform of a high German officer, he might be able in some way to order the sentries to allow our other men with dynamite to get in."

Tomaso looked puzzled for a moment, and then he understood. "You would like me to take a uniform for this man, so that he could wear it?" he asked.

"Yes, if you wouldn't endanger yourself in doing it," Dick said.

"Oh, even if there were danger," Tomaso said, "that would not bother me if it helped you. But there will not be any danger at all. I clean all the rooms. I am even alone in them sometimes. And they pay no attention to me, just an old man puttering around. They think I am not quite bright, anyway. I have made them think that my mind is almost gone, that I am a little imbecilic."

He chuckled, and the others smiled. How could the Germans ever hope to win against people like that?

"I know what uniform I shall take," Tomaso said, with a broad smile. "It should fit this man quite well, too. I shall take the uniform of the new Gestapo colonel who has set up headquarters here to search for that illegal radio everyone is talking about. He has many beautiful uniforms. He is a very vain man. And he is a very high official. Even the regular generals here are afraid of him—of the Gestapo!"

"Perfect!" Dick cried. "That couldn't be better!"

"Tomorrow night I shall have it for you," Tomaso said. "And I shall also be able to tell you then about the sabotage at the power plant. But come before eight o'clock. I do not want to miss any of the opera."

With a good-bye, Tomaso went back to his rooms, and the three Americans struck off for the northwestern road, which Dick was eager to look over. They kept to the side of the hill above the town so they would not be seen. In half an hour they came to the road where it cut into the hill above the gorge. They were able to get close to it, as the trees covered their approach.

"This road has been cut out of the hillside," Slade said. "It would be very easy to blow up. All you'd need would be a fair-sized charge behind some big rocks up here, and the side of the hill would just slide down on to the road. Of course, a good engineers' company could have it clear again in about four hours, with the proper equipment—bulldozers and such."

"The Germans won't have any such equipment by that time," Dick said. "It will all be under water. And a few hours is really all we need anyway. If they can't escape up this road, they'll be caught by the flood waters from the dam. The only way anyone could get away would be on foot into the hills. And that's just what we want."

"Then you're going to try to blow up this road?" Max asked.

"Yes, as my own private venture in this operation," Dick replied, "provided everything else works out all right. If I'm needed at the dam, then I'll forget this, but if our plans there look good, I'll come over here with the leftover dynamite."

They spent another half-hour on the hillside, looking over the land. Slade finally pointed out to Dick the best spot for placing his dynamite charge, and where he should stand with his detonator. Then the three men headed back behind the town and up to their cave on the opposite hill. It had been a busy night.

CHAPTER FOURTEEN

INTERRUPTED PERFORMANCE

They spent a good part of the next day sleeping, although they still had plenty of time to talk over their plans. They found it more difficult than ever to sit in front of the cave doing nothing when they knew so many things must be going on elsewhere. They wondered if the local tenor would succeed with his scheme of wrecking the dynamo. They asked each other a dozen times if old Tomaso would really be able to steal that Gestapo colonel's uniform. Max even spent some time practising his German, trying to get a note of authority and command into it.

"If I can just try to be as tough and nasty and mean as possible," he said, "then I may begin to sound a little bit like a Gestapo colonel."

"Well, you'll be talking to German soldiers," Scotti put in, "and you ought to find it easy to act nasty to them."

The lieutenant was much better now, and he could talk almost normally. There was a throbbing pain in his head regularly, and his broken leg was uncomfortable, but the thing that bothered him most was his inability to take any active part in the proceedings.

"You don't let me do anything, Dick," he protested. "It's you who figured out every plan so far, as well as carrying them through. I needn't have come along on this trip at all."

But Dick was relieved to be able to have the advice and counsel of his lieutenant in his complicated plans. Each one of them was a long gamble, and he knew it. He wanted the benefit of every bit of advice he could get. And it was Lieutenant Scotti who figured out the method Max was later to use in diverting the attention of the guards at the dam so that Slade could get in to place his dynamite.

That action was planned for that night—the fifth night of their stay behind the enemy lines. At dawn of the sixth night the dam was scheduled to be blown up, and they wanted to get their dynamite in place twenty-four hours ahead of time. Slade had figured that he could place the dynamite, run a wire down the pipe so that it extended about one inch from a hatch opening. Then, on the last night, he could hook up another length of wire to that, lead it away to his detonator, and set it off.

But they did not know that the Germans had decided there were Americans in the neighborhood. The decoding experts had not been able to decipher completely the radio messages which Tony had sent, but they had gotten enough of a hint to know that they were reports on German troop and supply

"I Didn't Need to Come Along," the Lieutenant Said

movements through Maletta. And they felt sure that military men were making those reports.

Dick Donnelly went off to town alone shortly after dark that evening. He was going to find out about the sabotage at the power plant and pick up the German uniform from Tomaso—that was all. Then he planned to return to the cave, where Max would put on the uniform, and they would all set out for the dam together.

There was nothing to worry him unduly as he circled over the fields and came up toward the villa on the north hill. He saw many trucks and cars on the road, but this was nothing new during the last few days. Just as he left the little dead-end side street and walked up the hill to meet Tomaso at the clump of trees, a car roared to a stop at the end of the street and German soldiers poured out of it, heading straight up the hill.

Dick ran forward quickly to the trees, and there he found Tomaso, nervous and agitated.

"It's terrible," the old man said. "You'll be caught!"

"What's terrible?" Dick asked. "What has happened?"

"I just learned—overheard the officers talking," Tomaso said. "They feel sure Americans are hiding somewhere in Maletta. They've surrounded the town and are going to search it thoroughly. They've got a ring around the town now, and it will close in

INTERRUPTED PERFORMANCE

more and more tightly as soldiers go through every house, every building."

"Oh—those soldiers who went up the hill over there—" Dick muttered. "They're part of the ring around the town."

"Yes, I heard them say men must circle up behind the villa, and then walk down so closely that not a person could slip through the ring. They'll be here any minute. We cannot stay here."

"No, come on down toward the villa," Dick said. "We can talk as we go. You have the uniform there?"

"Yes, shall I try to put it back now so we won't be caught with it?"

"No, I'll take it," Dick said. "I may be able to get away with it yet. What about the power plant?"

"The plan succeeded," Tomaso said. "The dynamo is wrecked, the water-gates shut, and specialists have been summoned from the north. But I hear they cannot arrive with new parts for at least three days."

"Good," Dick said.

"Not good," Tomaso said. "Of what use is all this if now you are to be caught?"

They were approaching the wing of the villa now, and hid in its shadow.

"I may not be caught," Dick said. "And even if I am, the others will carry through somehow. Has the guard been increased at the dam?"

"No, because they believe the damage was caused by a German workman," Tomaso said. "No Italians were there. So the German was judged careless and the Gestapo colonel had him brought down here at once. He ordered him shot. So the guard is not increased. Only a corporal is in charge at night. There are nine sentries under him."

They stopped and listened. Up above on the hill they heard the tramp of men's feet, the calling of orders in German.

"Come on," Dick said. "We might as well make them take as long as possible to find me. Where can we go?"

"I—I was going to the opera," Tomaso said. "I don't know now if I should go."

"Of course," Dick said. "You must not be found with me if I am caught. But wait—where is the opera house?"

"In the next block—to the right," Tomaso replied.

"Can we get there without crossing in front of the villa?" Dick asked.

"Yes, around in back," the old man said, grabbing his arm, "but we must hurry."

He led Dick behind the rear wing to the western side, cut behind a small house not far from the villa, brushed aside a dog who started to bark at the next house, and then stopped at a narrow street. Between two houses Dick could see what must be the opera house, a large building with numerous lights in it, and people already going in the front doors.

Dick hid the German uniform under his loose peasant's coat and spoke quietly to Tomaso.

"Take me to the stage door," he said. "Tell your tenor friend, the man who wrecked the power plant so cleverly, who I am. Then leave me. I have an idea."

They walked quickly across the street and along the side of the opera house to a side door near the rear. A man leaned against the doorjamb and looked up at them curiously.

"Arturo, quick," the old man said. "Ask no questions. Find Enrico at once. Bring him here."

The man's eyes opened wide, then he darted inside. He reappeared in a few seconds with a young man who limped slightly. The young man had begun to apply make-up to his face. He beckoned them inside.

"Enrico, this is the American," Tomaso said. "This is Ricardo Donnelli."

The young man looked at Dick in admiration but said nothing.

"The Germans have surrounded the town, and are searching for him," Tomaso said. "Help him. Do what he asks."

"Anything," Enrico said. "You go now, Tomaso."

The old man stopped at the door long enough to say, "Not a word of this," to the doorkeeper, who nodded his head in vigorous assent. Then he disappeared.

Dick spoke quickly in Italian to the young singer.

"I've got only one chance to escape detection," he said. "Let me play your role tonight. In the clown costume of *Pagliacci* they'll never recognize me. They'll just think I'm the regular tenor."

"Not if you sing as you used to," Enrico smiled. "You must be sure to sing very badly. Then you will sound like me."

"Perhaps the audience will know the difference," Dick said, "but I'll have to take a chance on that. Even if they do, maybe they will say nothing."

"They will say nothing," Enrico assured him. "They will know you are the American for whom the Germans search, and they will want to help you."

"What about those among you who work with the Germans?" Dick asked. "There are still some quislings, I believe."

"Yes, but they dare not come to public gatherings like this," Enrico said. "They are afraid of the rest of the townspeople."

"All right then?" Dick asked.

"All right," Enrico replied. "Come to my dressing room now. The others in the company must be told. They can be trusted, all of them. I shall tell them while you get into costume and make-up. Then I shall join the orchestra in the pit and play a drum inconspicuously."

In a few minutes Dick was putting the clown costume over his clothes. The floppy suit was so roomy that he was able to tie the Gestapo uniform around his waist beneath it. Then he smeared over his face the heavy dead-white make-up of the clown. When it dried, he put on his wig, and then the round red spots which covered the clown's face. He looked at himself in the cracked mirror.

"A mother couldn't recognize her own son in this get-up," he laughed. "I may be able to get away with this."

He heard a tap on his door and called "Come in," in Italian. A man in the costume of Tonio, with the fake hump on his back, entered the room and smiled.

"We all know," he said. "We shall help, no matter what happens. You are safe. And we shall never forget the great honor of having sung with—" then he decided he should never even mention the name, lest the Gestapo hear—"with the world's greatest tenor."

"Thanks," Dick said, with a smile. "I hope I won't get any of you into trouble."

While Tonio sang the prologue, Dick wondered what the men at the cave would be thinking. They expected him back there by this time. And what about Tony, still maintaining his lonely vigil in that old bell tower? He would have seen the Germans encircling the town, going through every house. It would be some little time before the searching parties would reach the opera house. It would be best if they came in while the performance was going on, and while Dick was on the stage.

Then someone called him, and he stood in the wings waiting for his cue. He looked about. The sets were old and dirty, as Tomaso had said. The stage was not very large. And the orchestra in the pit was about half as large as it used to be, Dick knew. But the men played as if they loved it, and the singers sang with fire and sincerity, even if their voices did not have the best quality in the world. He felt a thrill—a thrill he had not known for a long time—go through him as he heard the music and got himself ready to step on a stage once more and sing.

When he finally was there, singing, he knew that his voice was rusty, not up to its best by any means. But perhaps it was just as well. If he were in good voice, the Germans might make inquiries about him.

At the end of the first act there was a burst of applause that shook the old opera house, even though it was less than half filled. Between the acts, after taking his many bows, Dick was nervous. The audience obviously knew that he was not Enrico, the regular tenor. It was a big crowd to be in on something that was supposed to be so secret, but it was a chance he had had to take in view of developments. He kept listening for the approach of the searching German troops, hoping they would not come until the performance started again.

Finally there came the bell for the second act, and Dick as Canio went on the stage for his great aria, *Vesti la giubba*. It was in the midst of that sobbing, heartbroken song of the clown that Dick saw the Germans. They came in the front entrance of the opera house, about fifteen of them, led by the elegant but worried Gestapo colonel, who did not yet know, Dick concluded, that one of his uniforms had been stolen. Then Dick saw more soldiers in the wings, on both sides of the stage. But he kept on singing, as if nothing had happened. The Germans just stood and listened and, when he finished the aria, joined in the applause.

Dick bowed, and bowed again as the applause continued. But then the other singers started to go on with the performance. At that the colonel, with some of his men, strode down the hall holding up his hand for silence.

The singers stopped, and the orchestra drifted quickly into silence. The colonel then mounted the steps leading to the stage, strutting like a peacock. An aide followed him. When he was sure he had the attention of everyone, he uttered a few words in German to the aide, who thereupon spoke in Italian to the assemblage.

"His excellency begs your forgiveness for interrupting this beautiful performance," the man said in a toneless voice, "but he is compelled to do so because of spies in our fair city."

The aide paused while the colonel spoke more words to him in German. Then he continued to tell the audience that American spies were known to be somewhere in the town and a thorough, house-to-house search had to be made for them. The colonel was sure, the aide said, that only a few of the Italian population would think of harboring such criminals, and that most of them would aid in running down their common enemy. He then asked if anyone knew of the whereabouts of any American spy.

No one raised a hand. The colonel then said it would be necessary for his men to go through the entire theater carefully looking for the Americans. As soon as the search was ended, the performance could continue. At that, German soldiers moved down the aisles, asking everyone for papers, for some means of identification if they had lost their papers. Others went through the orchestra pit, the dressing rooms, the basement, and the catwalk above the stage where sets were pulled up out of sight.

The colonel waited on the stage while all this was going on. Dick and the others stood on the stage not far from him, waiting until everything was over. No one thought of asking the singers for identification papers. No one paid any attention to them except the colonel, who rather self-consciously smiled at them a couple of times.

INTERRUPTED PERFORMANCE 219

In half an hour the search was ended, and the colonel looked a little worried as he told his aide to say that anyone knowing of the presence of an American should report it to headquarters at once.

As the Germans moved toward the exits, Dick motioned to the orchestra leader, who raised his baton, and took up where he had left off. In a few minutes there were no more soldiers, and the ring closing in on the American spies had passed beyond them. Dick sang the rest of his role with a happiness and a fervor such as he had never felt. His singing inspired the other performers and the orchestra to new heights of beauty.

Shortly before the end he had an idea.

He knew all these people in the opera house could be trusted now. So he would take this opportunity to tell them of the impending destruction of the dam. Following the music of the orchestra but making up new words as he went along, he thanked them all for their help, assured them they would soon be liberated by the American Army. He told them when the dam would be blown up, told them to leave the town before that time, filtering out into the hills as unobtrusively as possible.

At the end of the passage in which he told them these things, one of the other singers sang his part and also invented words for the music. He said that the Americans could count on full cooperation of the people of Maletta, who would return from the hills to welcome the conquering American Army.

Soon the opera ended, and the applause was deafening. After many bows, Dick left the stage and hurried to his dressing room. There he found Enrico, and soon Tomaso came. He hardly listened to their praise of his voice, of his cleverness in using the opera to tell the townspeople of the plans ahead. But, when he had removed the make-up and costume, he shook Enrico by the hand heartily.

"You have been a tremendous help," he said, "in more ways than one. First the dam, then this. The whole American Army will thank you, Enrico, believe me!"

Then he and Tomaso were gone. They left the side door of the opera house, cut back of the villa, and then Dick went up on the roof and into the tower with Tony. There he told the whole story to to the young radioman, who had been fearful that something must have gone wrong.

"Why couldn't I have heard you?" he asked. "I'm missing everything imprisoned up in this tower—most of the war, and now your singing!"

"Well, I'm going to sit down for a few minutes," Dick said. "We can't carry through our plan to go to the dam tonight. It's too late for me to get back to the cave, get Max into his uniform, carry the dynamite to the dam and place it. It will just have to be done tomorrow night. So I'll stay here until our one o'clock broadcast to headquarters and help you with it."

"No you won't," Tony said. "You've had one narrow escape tonight. After this broadcast, they'll have their mobile units out trying to find us. They may throw another dragnet around the city, because that Colonel Klage will be just about crazy. I'll handle this one alone. You get on back to the cave and let those boys up there stop biting their nails for fear something's gone wrong. I don't care if you are my sergeant and I'm only a corporal. You get out of here—right now!"

Dick grinned and shook his head. "All right, all right," he said. "I guess you're right at that. You know what to tell them in your report. Good luck! I'll see you sometime tomorrow night."

CHAPTER FIFTEEN

NO CALM BEFORE THE STORM

The men at the cave were doing far more than biting their nails. They were pacing up and down, those who could, and Scotti was just about to send Vince and Max off to town to see what had happened.

When Dick walked in, he had so many questions hurled at him at once that he could say nothing at all. Finally he got everyone calmed down, and they sat down on the floor of the cave near Scotti while he told the whole story of the exciting evening. As he got into it, he was not interrupted once, for they all listened with open mouths at the almost incredible story he had to relate.

"And so," he concluded, "I saw it was really too late to get to the dam tonight. It would be dangerous. We might not be finished before it began to grow light, and that would be just too bad."

"It shouldn't take too long at the dam," Slade said. "I think I can rig everything in half an hour if Vince can help me carry the stuff into the pipe."

"I know, but we've got to allow for all emergencies," Dick said, "for delays like the one that happened to me tonight."

"Yes, Dick's right," Scotti agreed. "That dam operation is one that can't be rushed. If everything goes well you can be through in half an hour, yes. But what if there's a slip-up? What if that other colonel appears in the midst of things, for instance? There are any number of things that might happen to make you lie low for a few hours. And, anyway, I was never too sure about getting everything in there a full day before we were to set it off. We can do it on the last night, all right. Now you boys all get some sleep. You'll be needing it."

After a bite to eat from their tins they went to sleep, but all of them dreamed of explosions, of bridges being blown up, of dangerous parachute jumps, or something involving action and danger. The first light of dawn found them all awake, brewing some coffee over a small fire.

And then there was the whole day to pass. They did it by going over their plans endlessly, until they themselves were almost tired of talking about them.

"This is a dull day, all right," Vince complained. "I guess it's the calm before the storm."

"There'll be no calm before our storm," Dick said. "The storm starts a few minutes before dawn tomorrow, and we're going to have a mighty busy night before that time comes."

"And I guess we won't be able to sit down and have a siesta right *after* the storm, either," Max added.

As it began to grow dark, Max got into his beautiful German uniform. The others admired him greatly as he strutted about in front of the cave trying hard to act like a Gestapo colonel.

"Say—I just thought of something," he said. "As a big shot I wouldn't be traveling around without a staff or a few orderlies."

"It is a little unusual," Scotti said. "But you're out to check up on things personally. You're dropping in on sentries without any warning. In our Army, a private, or even a corporal, might wonder about such a thing, but German soldiers aren't taught to wonder. They don't bother to think, especially in the presence of a high officer. And with the plan we've got arranged they won't have time to think much."

"All right," Max said. "I just hope these guys react the way we expect them to."

"If they don't, you all know what to do," Scotti said. "I don't like the idea of gunfire at this crucial moment, but if we have to—well, we have to."

They set off about nine o'clock, leaving Scotti alone in the cave. He was propped up near the entrance with a sub-machine gun across his knees, two others near at hand, and several boxes of ammunition within reach. After the others had left, he looked through the darkness after them for a long time. Then he angrily brushed away the tears that kept coming into his eyes, and reached out and

Scotti Looked After the Others

banged his broken leg.

"Why did that leg have to break?" he demanded. "I ought to be there with my men and here I sit—"

But he stopped and gained control of himself again. Dick Donnelly could carry this thing through if anyone could. He had shown amazing cleverness so far in this matter, even when things got the most dangerous.

Dick was not feeling as confident, however. He felt pretty tired, and this test ahead of him was almost too much for him to carry. It was even worse, almost, to know that your commanding officer expected so much of you, to know that the men under you would do just about anything you said.

They all carried heavy loads—the entire batch of dynamite, lengths of wire, detonator boxes. But they made their way around the hill all right, and came down toward the dam from above, as they had before. Dick went ahead and looked up and down the main road, motioned to the others, and they sprinted across, dropping into the ditch on the other side. Then they slipped down the steep slope toward the power house below the dam. The grass grew high here, and they were able to pile up the dynamite and other equipment not far from the big pipe-line. Then Max and Dick climbed up to the road again.

"All right, now, Max," Dick said. "I'll cut around below the power house and cross to the other side of the dam. Give me about three minutes' head start.

After that, wait for the next car that comes along. Just after it passes walk down this little drive toward the dam wall. The sentries are likely to think you got out of the car they heard. But don't give them a chance to think much. Bawl them out, raise the devil, call the guards down below at the power house and get them to come up to you. Then you'll have them all together when I open fire. I'll be back in the woods on the other side of the lake. I'll be able to see, by the lights near that little building on the dam wall, when you have them all around you. I'll give a good burst on the gun and then light out as fast as I can. You send them after me."

"Okay, Dick," Max said. "I'll do my best. And I'll follow behind them too, to keep them looking for you. I'll give Slade and Vince a full half-hour, longer if possible."

Dick went quickly down the hill, alongside the road. He ducked into the ditch when a row of big trucks raced by, toward Maletta. Finally he left the roadside and cut down into the valley, about a quarter of a mile below the power house. He made his way across the trickling brook which was almost dry now that the water gates were shut. Then he headed up toward the dam again on the other side.

Vince and Slade were hiding by their supplies in the tall grass. They saw three sentries around the power house, five more pacing the dam wall. They would be able to see when Max walked out there, acting like a Nazi.

The wait seemed interminable. Then they heard a car go by on the road above them, and there was Max, striding vigorously out on to the dam wall. The nearest sentry snapped to attention and saluted, muttering a command back to the others as he did so. They all came to attenion, and Max started bellowing orders.

Vince and Slade could not understand him, but they smiled at each other over the rough sound of Max's voice. And it was obvious that the sentries were pretty scared. One of them jumped to the door of the little building and out came two more guards, hurriedly buttoning their jackets. At this sight, Max seemed to fly into a rage, and he slapped both the men hard across their faces. Then he called to the men farther along on the dam and they raced forward, snapped to attention in front of Max, and saluted.

Vince shot a glance at the sentries around the power house. They were staring up toward the wall, and whispering to each other. At that moment, Max looked down at them and bellowed an order that sounded so severe it almost made Slade quake in his boots. The three power-house sentries ran forward, climbed the steel ladder that led up to the dam and stood at attention before Max.

"He's got 'em all lined up," Vince whispered. "Every one of 'em. It's going to work."

"Right," Slade said, "and I've got our hatch in the pipe-line picked out."

Then they heard Dick's automatic firing from across the lake. The sentries on the dam were already so scared that they almost jumped off when they heard the sound. After all, one man in the power house had been shot that afternoon for neglect and carelessness, and by the very Gestapo officer, they thought, who now stood before them.

Max rasped out another order, and the sentries started running across the dam wall to the other side of the lake, with Max on their heels. In a flash Slade and Vince were out of the tall grass, running forward toward the pipe-lines, each with a heavy load. Slade took a wrench from his pocket and started work on the hatch opening in the pipe while Vince ran back for another load of material. By the time he returned, Slade had the door open and was boosting himself inside.

Vince handed up one big bundle to Slade, who disappeared with it inside the pipe. Then Vince kept his eyes sweeping over the surrounding land, looking for any sign that someone might approach. Inside the big pipe, Slade was struggling up the sloping steel shaft toward the dam wall. He slipped, he fell, but he picked himself up again and pushed forward. It took him five minutes to reach the end of the pipe, where the water-gate of the dam stopped him. Here he set down his load, turned, and slid down the pipe to the opening, dousing his flashlight before he got there.

Vince was ready for him with the next bundle. This was even heavier, and it took Slade almost ten minutes to get it in position. When he slid down again, one hand was cut and his knees were badly skinned, but he grabbed the coil of wire which Vince handed him and started up again.

Meanwhile, after firing his shots over the lake, Dick had run full speed toward the west, back toward the dam. He had to get past the dam wall before the sentries came racing from it. He heard their pounding feet close at hand just as he slid into a clump of low bushes just below the dam wall. He could hear Max roaring out his orders and he knew that the supposed colonel was ordering the sentries to go to the right, up along the lake, in search of the man who had fired the shots. They all obeyed without question, and then Dick slipped away from the bushes, went down the hill alongside the stream, crossed over, and cut back up to the spot beside the power house at which he had left Vince and Slade.

He smiled as he saw that the hatch door was open in the pipe-line, with Vince standing guard beside it. He whistled a signal and stepped forward out of the tall grass.

"He's hooking up the wire now," Vince whispered to him. "Ought to be down in a minute."

And then Slade, appearing at the opening, leaped

to the ground. He had the coil of wire over his arm and was letting it out as he moved away from the dynamite charge at the base of the dam gates. He nodded briefly to Dick, then closed the hatch door, but not so tight that it would cut through the wire. He stepped back toward the tall grass swiftly, still paying out his wire.

Dick and Vince followed him, helping him up the steep slope toward the road. He was heading for a culvert which passed under the road about fifty feet west of the little driveway to the dam wall. He did not even pause as he ducked low and started crawling through the culvert. Dick went up on the road, scurried across and got at the other end of the opening. He could barely see Slade's flashlight as he made his way through the small tunnel.

After he was through, Vince came across and joined them, and then they made their way up the hill on the other side of the road, into the thick trees.

"Here," Slade said, panting, "this will be the place. Vince, go get the detonator."

"I'll go with you," Dick said. "I want to get my own stuff, too."

While Slade sat down to rest, Dick and Vince went back across the road, into the tall grass where they had first put their heavy bundles. There were two detonators, a box of fuses, a length of wire, and one big box of dynamite. They picked them up and hurried back to join Slade. When they reached him again, they were all exhausted, but happy. There was still no sign of Max or his sentries, who were busy, apparently, chasing through the woods on the other side of the dam and lake.

They sat and waited, secure in the knowledge that now the dam would really be blown up. The charge was laid, the fuses set, the wire hooked up. At the proper moment Slade would just have to push down a plunger, and the dam would be ruined, flood waters would roar down into the valley below, engulfing the German forces and their mighty armored equipment.

Meanwhile, in the country around the town of Maletta, there were many strange sights. Since dark, Italian families had been starting out for short strolls, strolls that led down side streets and then up paths into the wooded hills. They took different streets, different roads, and they walked slowly, casually, whistling or humming songs as they walked. Some carried bundles, and some even took their babies out, when they should have been in their cribs asleep.

But only a few of the Germans seemed to notice. Most of them were too busy to see anything like Italians taking a stroll. An aide did mention to the Gestapo colonel that there seemed to be an unusual number of Italians out on the streets that evening, but the colonel was in no mood to listen. He had just discovered one of his newest uniforms to be missing and he was berating an orderly with its loss. Moreover, he had still not located that illegal radio, and his commanding officer had ordered him to appear before him the next day with a full explanation.

Far into the night the imperceptible exodus of Italians from the town went on, and nobody said a word. Tomorrow the Germans expected the big smashing attack from the Americans who were now only ten miles below Maletta.

Another wanderer on those hills was Dick Donnelly. He carried a coil of wire over his shoulder, a box of dynamite in one hand, and a detonator in the other. Vince had begged to be allowed to go with him, but Dick would not listen.

"This is my own private venture," he said, "this blowing up of the road. I'll endanger my own life in it, but nobody else's. The dam is the important thing. You stay here with Slade and Max until it is all over, then head back for the cave fast."

Max had reappeared just before Dick left. After three-quarters of an hour hunting some fugitive in the woods, he led his sentries back to the dam. And he was fuming. He let forth a stream of abuse that would have made the real Colonel Klage envious. He blamed everything that had gone wrong in the war on those sentries, threatened to have them up for punishment the next day.

He gave a final order for them all to stay on the dam wall the rest of the night, and to keep their eyes constantly on the other side of the lake. Then he stalked away. The sentries were lined up like wooden Indians, facing the other direction. They couldn't have seen as far as the main road anyway, to see that Max just ducked across it into the woods above, but they didn't even dare try to see.

Max was proud and happy. "I ran the legs off those guys," he said. "And it did me good to hit a couple of them, too. They like to go around doing that kind of thing to people who can't hit back. I wonder how they liked a taste of their own medicine."

Dick told Max what a fine job he had done, but the big soldier just said, "I guess I'll go in for acting after I get out of the Army. It's fun."

CHAPTER SIXTEEN

ZERO HOUR

Tony Avella was nearing the end of his long vigil in the top of the bell tower. He was feeling restless, cramped, and uneasy. He kept telling himself that this radio job was just as important as any of the rest of it, but it did not make him feel any better about having to spend almost a whole week in that cramped space, hot in the day, cold at night, with a stone floor beneath him. Most of the time he had nothing whatever to do, and he had covered the floor with scratches playing tick-tack-toe with himself.

But now the end was approaching. It had been some time since he'd heard about the latest plans, but he knew that the dam was scheduled to go up at exactly five-thirty A.M. And he thought that Dick was going to try to get around to the northwest road to blow it up at the same time.

"At any rate, I've got box seats for the whole affair," he told himself. "I'll be able to see both explosions from here. But I can't wait around very long after that."

Although there was still a half-hour to wait, he sat down beside his radio and felt for the cranks of the generator. He put on the earphones and took them off, adjusted the microphone before his mouth and then moved it a half inch further away. Then it was time to look at his watch again, the watch that he felt sure must be running down.

"Wonder where Dick is now," he said to himself.

Dick was almost as nervous as Tony. He sat behind a huge boulder above the northwest road where it was cut into the side of the hill. He had laid his charge just where Slade showed him, and hooked up the fuses and wire. Now he sat waiting beside the plunger box for five-thirty to come.

"I hope everything's still okay at the dam," he muttered to himself.

Except for nervousness again, everything *was* all right there. Max and Slade and Vince sat on the side of the hill, looking at their watches, laughing about the sentries who still stood on the dam wall, looking at their watches again.

"Scotti must be kind of lonesome," Vince said.

Lieutenant Scotti was *very* lonesome. The night had been particularly long for him, with nothing whatever to do, without any way of knowing how the affair at the dam had gone. He looked at his watch.

"Pretty soon I'll hear it," he said to himself. "Then I'll know the answer. And Tony will flash word to headquarters at once."

At that moment Tony was beginning to turn the crank on the generator. He got it going at a steady pace and kept it going easily. Then he turned a switch, looked at his watch. Any minute now—

He jumped when it finally did come, after all those hours of waiting. A great roar to the east. He saw a flash, saw black smoke against the sky that was beginning to be gray, felt the earth tremble a little, and then heard the booming roar go echoing through the hills.

But—was that an echo? No, it was another roar, though not so loud, from the west. Looking quickly, he saw a cloud of smoke and dust rising from the northwest road.

"Julius Caesar to Mark Antony!" he cried into the microphone. And he got the answer back right away, "Mark Antony to Julius Caesar. Come in."

He did not bother with code. He was not going to say anything that the Germans wouldn't know in two minutes anyway.

"Dam blown up at five-thirty on the dot," he said swiftly. "Northwest road ditto one minute later. Repeat."

The man at the other end repeated the news once, and Tony was on his feet. He tossed the headphones and microphone to the floor, threw the rope out the opening and let himself over the ledge. Sliding down it like a streak of lightning, his feet hit the roof of the wing, and he ran in a crouch to the rear. He leaped to the ground and stumbled—into Tomaso's arms.

"Uncle Tomaso," he cried. "Why aren't you in the hills?"

"I couldn't go and leave you here, Tony," the old man said. "I had to make sure that you were safe."

"Come with me, fast," Tony said. "We have to hurry to get across the road before the water is too deep."

They took off through the trees, not bothering to hide themselves too carefully. They could hear the shouts from men in front of the villa, the firing of a few guns, the sound of motorcar engines roaring to life. Everyone would be too busy to notice them.

"Dick's got even further to go than we have," Tony said, as he trotted beside the old man, who could not move very quickly. "I wonder if he can make it."

Dick had known that it would not be easy for him to get back to the cave after blowing up the road. It had been a great thrill for him to see the hillside go sliding down across the highway, obliterating it completely for a stretch of a quarter of a mile. But he had lost his own footing and gone rolling down the hill too. Before he caught himself, he was almost at the road, and there, just in front of him, was a German motorcycle messenger pulling up to a screaming stop in front of the mass of rocks that blocked his way.

Dick did not hesitate for an instant. He snatched his automatic from his pocket, fired, and watched the man topple to the ground.

"I'm afraid I'm a little too excited to be a good shot," he told himself critically. "I believe I just winged him in the shoulder."

But that was enough for Dick's purpose. He pulled up the man's motorcycle, turned it around, started it, and headed straight down the main highway for Maletta. He roared down the main street at forty miles an hour, swerving in and out among the cars, the trucks, the running soldiers with half their clothes on. The sight of such panic made him laugh with pleasure, and everything was in such a turmoil that he was able to race right through the heart of town without being noticed except as a nuisance that got in someone's way.

"They don't even know, half of them, what's happened yet," he told himself as he sped out again on the northeast road. "But they'll know mighty soon," he added, "for there comes the water."

His motorcycle wheels were already running in water an inch deep. Then it was six inches, eight inches, ten inches. Ahead he saw it boiling down at him like a solid wall, and he leaped from the motorcycle and cut into the fields. The mud and water slowed him down but he raced ahead as fast as he could. Another fifty feet, another thirty! The water was around his knees. Twenty feet—ten feet to go to high ground—and the water was around his waist. And then he made it. He grabbed the trunk of a sapling and pulled himself up the slope. Then he sat down, panting heavily. But in another minute his feet were in the steadily rising water, and he pulled himself up again.

"Anyway," he told himself, "I know the dam really went out. It's not just cracked and leaking."

Breathing a little more easily, he got up and started up the hill toward the cave. Halfway up he heard the firing of guns. The sound came from the cave without a doubt. He ran forward, circling around to come at the cave from above if possible. He figured that he must be just a little above the cave entrance when he heard another burst of fire and heard a bullet *zing* through the branches overhead. He dropped to the ground and edged his way down the slope on his belly, keeping behind trees as much as possible. He knew there was a big tree growing out of a split rock just above the cave entrance. If only he could get to that—

"Scotti must be alone in there," he said. "And— yes, I can see them—they're German soldiers who have come racing up the hill to get away from the flood waters. They probably would have run smack into the cave by accident if Scotti hadn't fired to keep them off. I've got to get down to him."

After each burst of fire from the German guns he made his way forward another few feet, keeping always behind tree trunks. Finally he reached the great tree just above the cave entrance. Then he

Dick Stopped Behind a Tree and Waited

waited again. There was another heavy exchange of fire and a lull. With one leap, Dick flew down from above, hit the ground and fell on Scotti's gun just as he was about to pull the trigger.

"Dick!" he cried. "I almost plugged you!"

"I didn't give you a chance," Dick said. He crouched low as a hail of bullets spat against the side of the hill all around the cave. He snatched up one of the machine guns by Scotti's side and returned the fire.

"We can hold 'em off for a long time," Dick said. "We've got a lot of ammunition."

"Until they think to circle up in back the way you did," Scotti said. "Dick, you're a fool to have come back here. I'm done for, anyway, but you can get away. Our men must be right over the crest of the hill. You can get up to them all right."

"Nothing doing," Dick said. "I'm sticking with you."

"That's plain suicide!" Scotti fumed. "As your superior officer I order you to leave."

Dick just laughed as they both gave another burst of fire toward the Germans who continued their forward creeping toward the entrance of the cave.

"You're not my superior officer right now," he said to Scotti. "You're completely incapacitated and I'm acting commander of this outfit and you know it. You told me so yourself. So I order Sergeant Dick Donnelly to stay right here and keep shooting

German soldiers."

There was no more fire from the enemy, however. A long pause followed, and Dick and Scotti glanced at each other wonderingly.

"You know what that means," Scotti said.

"I'm afraid so," Dick replied. "They've sent some men up to come in from above, the way I did."

"Help me to the back of the cave," Scotti said. "We can plug them as they try to come in. At least we can get them before they get a bead on us. They can't see clear in to the back."

"That'll be all right for a while," Dick said, pulling Scotti backward. "Until they can use the bodies of their own dead as a shield."

They settled themselves against the rear of the cave with their guns and ammunition beside them. And at that moment four German soldiers were approaching the big tree above the cave entrance.

Just as the first man was about to leap, there was a burst of fire from behind him. He toppled forward, and Dick and Scotti had the pleasure of seeing a wounded German fall flat at the cave entrance, without their having moved a muscle.

The other Germans above the cave turned, just in time to meet another burst of fire from a gun in the hands of Max Burckhardt. They fell without having a chance to fire, and Max, followed by Vince and Slade, rushed forward.

"Scotti!" they called. "Scotti!"

Dick ran to the cave entrance and called out to the men above, "Look out! There still may be some more in the woods below."

But no shot came from there, and Max, Vince, and Slade scrambled down the hill into the cave.

"What kept you so long?" Dick asked.

"Well, first we waited to see just what went on at the dam," Vince said. "It went out—every bit of it—dam, power house, water, and all! It was beautiful to watch. And then on the way back here we ran into a few Germans. We didn't have any guns ourselves, but we sort of took them by surprise and handled them with bare knuckles. That's where Max picked up the gun he used on the fellow that was about to visit you. Only one of the Germans we met had a gun and that's it. The others were so panicky because of the flood that they'd forgotten them. But that little tussle delayed us a bit. Sorry."

"Wonder where Tony is?" Dick mumbled. But before anyone had time to answer they heard the pounding of many feet. They grabbed up guns and waited at the entrance tensely. Then Vince let out a war whoop that rang through the woods.

"It's our boys!" he shouted. "It's our own Army!"

CHAPTER SEVENTEEN

AFTERMATH

They were all in the town of Maletta again, two months later. It looked cleaner and neater than when they had first seen it, for the townspeople and the U. S. Army engineers had done a first-rate job of cleaning out the mud and trash left by the flood waters.

Scotti was back in the United States, recuperating from his wounds, but the rest of them were heading back to the front lines again, quite a distance to the north by this time. They took the last day of their furlough for a visit in the town that had been so important a part of their lives for one week.

But there were some differences. Dick Donnelly wore a First Lieutenant's bars on his shoulders. The General had conferred the commissioned rank on him on the field of action, right after the successful conclusion of the battle for Maletta. And there was the colored ribbon on his left breast which meant the awarding of the Distinguished Service Medal.

Tony Avella was a Master Sergeant now. He and his Uncle Tomaso had been caught on the opposite hill, away from the cave, by the flood waters. But that had meant nothing more than sitting and waiting for the waters to recede. They had been hungry and exhausted after their ordeal but that was all. Even old Tomaso stood up well under it.

Vince Salamone and Max Burckhardt were both corporals now and everyone in the group had some sort of citation in recognition of his brilliant and heroic work. Boom-Boom Slade, as meek and quiet as always, seemed a little embarrassed at the decoration on his breast.

They all went to call on old Tomaso first of all. They found him in his same old room in the servants' wing, but not the sad and broken man they had first seen there. He had put on a little weight, decent clothes now enhanced his dignified bearing. With characteristic Italian emotion he gratefully saluted the American flag which now flew above the door of the ancient villa.

"Did they take down the radio from the tower?" Tony asked him.

"No, it's still there," Tomaso said. "I think they may just have forgotten about it. And I haven't said anything because when this war is over I want the town to put that in a museum—as a memorial to the battle of Maletta."

"Well, it can stay there for all I care," Tony said. "I had my fill of that bell tower for the rest of my life. I never want to see it again."

Tomaso led them to a sidewalk restaurant where they sat and drank coffee and talked together. They recalled all their experiences again, reliving in memory those hectic days. It was a good memory, and the result had been a great success. Thousands of German soldiers had been drowned, thousands more killed by the Americans that poured across the two ridges and so caught them in a vise. Hundreds of trucks and tanks and guns had been lost by the enemy and many of these were already repaired and serving the American forces. The general told them that their work had saved at least a month in the Italian campaign, probably more.

While they sat, Enrico came along and said hello to them all.

"Now," he said to Dick, "I can take time to ask you for your autograph."

Dick felt foolish, but he signed a note for the young Italian. Enrico thanked the young lieutenant profusely, and then said very seriously,

"You know the opera company is singing *Cavalleria Rusticana* tonight. I'm really not up to it. It would be a great treat for me to sit in the audience. How about it, Ricardo Donnelli, will you sing *Turridu* tonight?"

"Bravo," cried Tomaso with a wave of his hand and his black eyes sparkling. "The great Donnelli it is for tonight."

"No, no," Dick protested. "I'm not a singer these days, I'm a soldier."

"Forget it, big boy," exclaimed Vince Salamone

with affection and not without humor, for he was a good foot taller than Dick. "You're going to be *Turridu* tonight and capture the hearts of all the girls in Maletta."

"You bet you are," agreed Tony. "He's my favorite opera hero, and I'd like to hear his role sung proper-like." Adding with a mock-serious bow to Enrico, "No offense to you, my good fellow."

And Max Burckhardt exclaimed in his good-natured way, "No kiddin', Lieutenant. I'd like to find out first hand if all the hullabaloo I hear about those vocal chords of yours is on the level."

Boom-Boom Slade came out of his customary reticence to add, "It would give me the keenest pleasure, Lieutenant Donnelly, to hear a man sing whose talents as a soldier I so deeply respect."

So that evening they all went to see Ricardo Donnelli in *Cavalleria Rusticana*. But the next morning it was Lieutenant Dick Donnelly that reported to his commanding officer at the front lines.

WHITMAN
AUTHORIZED EDITIONS

NEW STORIES OF ADVENTURE AND MYSTERY

Up-to-the-minute novels for boys and girls about Favorite Characters, all popular and well-known, including—

INVISIBLE SCARLET O'NEIL
LITTLE ORPHAN ANNIE and the Gila Monster Gang
BRENDA STARR, Girl Reporter
DICK TRACY, Ace Detective
TILLIE THE TOILER and the Masquerading Duchess
BLONDIE and Dagwood's Adventure in Magic
BLONDIE and Dagwood's Snapshot Clue
BLONDIE and Dagwood's Secret Service
JOHN PAYNE and the Menace at Hawk's Nest
BETTY GRABLE and the House With the Iron Shutters
BOOTS (of "Boots and Her Buddies") and the Mystery of the Unlucky Vase
ANN SHERIDAN and the Sign of the Sphinx
JANE WITHERS and the Swamp Wizard

The books listed above may be purchased at the same store where you secured this book.

WHITMAN
AUTHORIZED EDITIONS

JANE WITHERS and the Phantom Violin
JANE WITHERS and the Hidden Room
BONITA GRANVILLE and the Mystery of Star Island
ANN RUTHERFORD and the Key to Nightmare Hall
POLLY THE POWERS MODEL: The Puzzle of the Haunted Camera
JOYCE AND THE SECRET SQUADRON: A Captain Midnight Adventure
NINA AND SKEEZIX (of "Gasoline Alley"): The Problem of the Lost Ring
GINGER ROGERS and the Riddle of the Scarlet Cloak
SMILIN' JACK and the Daredevil Girl Pilot
APRIL KANE AND THE DRAGON LADY: A "Terry and the Pirates" Adventure
DEANNA DURBIN and the Adventure of Blue Valley
DEANNA DURBIN and the Feather of Flame
GENE AUTRY and the Thief River Outlaws
RED RYDER and the Mystery of the Whispering Walls
RED RYDER and the Secret of Wolf Canyon

The books listed above may be purchased at the same store where you secured this book.

THE EXCITING NEW
FIGHTERS FOR FREEDOM SERIES

Thrilling novels of war and adventure for modern boys and girls

Kitty Carter of the CANTEEN CORPS

Nancy Dale, ARMY NURSE

March Anson and Scoot Bailey of the U.S. NAVY

Dick Donnelly of the PARATROOPS

Norma Kent of the WACS

Sally Scott of the WAVES

Barry Blake of the FLYING FORTRESS

Sparky Ames and Mary Mason of the FERRY COMMAND

The books listed above may be purchased at the same store where you secured this book.